Forbidden & Taboo Explicit Sex Stories

Adult Erotica Collection - BDSM, Virgins, Gangbangs, 69, Lesbian, First Time, Anal, Threesomes, MILFs, Spanking, Creampies (Orgasmic Collection)

Written By:
G.G. Goode

- Goode Publications -

Contents

The Meadows High School gym was packed nearly elbow-to-elbow with well-dressed men and women in their late twenties. They were all well-dressed in formal, and business attire. A sparkling banner advertising the class of 2009's ten-year reunion was stretched across the school gym's entrance, and balloons bounced against the tall ceiling, as if they were trying to escape. People bustled and moved through the bunched-up lines, seemingly eager to get inside. The room was loud with various conversations and pop music from ten years ago playing in the background. All the former classmates curiously inspected each other's lives to see how accurate the yearbook's "most likely to" predictions turned out to be. They all sized each other up, hoping that they could appear more successful than the next. Groups of former friends began to form into cliques just like it had been when they attended the school. It was all very nostalgic for many, and terrifying for others.

At the edge of the room stood the smallest of all the groups, just two women that not many of the other reunion-goers could remember. Dayna and Ella were not popular back then by any means, so it did not surprise them that most of the other alumni could not recall them at all. For the first time, everyone in the room seemed almost obsessively interested in who they were. Their former classmates finally started taking interest in them, probably because they noticed their striking appearances, high-dollar clothes, perfect bodies, and Hollywood style. These ladies had clearly risen above the housewife status that most of the women in this room had achieved. Other women speculated and gossiped about who they must be, spreading rumors just to make themselves appear relevant. Several men had tried to offer the ladies a drink, as they flirted and gawked at them relentlessly. The two women had been close friends in school, and they seemed to be reconnecting seamlessly, ignoring everyone's attempts at making conversation, in the same way they had once been ignored.

Dayna and Ella chatted briefly before both grew tired of the class reunion. After all, they only came to see each other, and they had no interest in being gawked at or even spoken to by anyone else in this room. They both got in their cars and drove to the closest open bar they could find. It was a little sleazy, but they had agreed that it would be better than spending the whole night searching for something more suitable. The only alternative was driving hours to get to some place decent, so they settled on Mike's Hole-in-the-Wall, which had bar food that was far greater than what you would usually expect from a place like this. They sat at a high-top table near the bar and they each ordered their favorite martinis. The conversation began with polite chatter, and typical niceties, but that did not last exceedingly long. They learned the basics of each other's lives. Dayna shared photos of her only son, and Ella complained about her competitive career. With each drink they grew more and more comfortable and the conversation became increasingly personal. They began guiltlessly prodding one another for the most exciting and personal details of their lives. Just like they had when they met the first time, they became fast friends.

Dayna giggled uncontrollably as a bit of her drink sloshed over the rim of her martini glass and fell onto the table. She was having a great time catching up with Ella, her best friend from high school. It felt good because it had been a long time since she had had someone who she considered to be a real friend. They both used to be the outcasts in school. Both made good grades and always had a book in their hands, they went through a gothic phase together which did not do much for their social status. Other than by each other, and maybe a few teachers, they were hardly ever noticed when they walked through the halls. They both dressed dark and mostly plain back then. Dayna had an acne problem, long dirty blonde hair, and always kept her hair tied back. Ella was a tall brunette who hid behind thick-rimmed glasses. Their old selves probably would not recognize the people they were now. Now Dayna's hair was bleached and cut in a short choppy cut which accentuated her jaw line, and tattoos decorated much of her exposed skin. The red heels she wore highlighted her long legs, and her voluptuous lips were painted a matching red as well. Ella's hair was pinned into a fancy updo. Her low-cut top boasted her recently acquired fake boobs, which accentuated her hourglass figure perfectly.

"Oh my god! I can't believe it finally happened, I thought you were never going to give up your virginity!", Dayna exclaimed excitedly.

Ella scoffed as she noticed heads turning from almost every seat in the low-key bar. "Yeah, I know", she rolled her eyes and smirked in a way that indicated she was proud of the feat. "College definitely helped me grow up a lot!", she declared after gulping down the last of her drink. She waved at the bartender for another.

"Oh, come on spill it, Ella", Dayna pushed. "I told you how it happened for me already, so I want to hear your story".

"Alright, I'll tell it", Ella said. "But you gotta tell me a juicy one in return", She bartered.

"Deal", Dayna said firmly and without a second thought.

Ella's lips formed a mischievous grin as she remembered her deflowering. She squirmed a little in her seat and felt her pussy get a bit wet from thinking about it. She began telling Dayna every detail of how it happened.

Ella's First Steamy College Lesson (virginity)

She stumbled through the huge double doors relieved that she had made it just in time. Ella looked around the huge auditorium-like classroom. Hoping to avoid being noticed or called on, she chose a seat that seemed inconspicuous a few rows back from the front of the room and towards the middle of the row. After taking her seat, she clumsily rummaged through her brown shoulder bag, and got out her English textbook, and a purple spiral notebook labeled *English Notes*. She scooped up a handful of ballpoint pens, highlighters, and mechanical pencils before dropping her bag to the floor and used the sides of her sneakers to push the bag completely under the padded metal chair she sat on. She suddenly felt a light tap on her shoulder which made her jump a little.

"Did you sign in?", a deep smooth voice had asked.

Ella turned and looked towards the voice. There stood an extremely attractive guy. He could not be much older than she was. She could see his muscular form through the light blue button up he wore, pieces of his light brown hair fell into his face slightly covering one of his eyes. He pushed the hair out of his huge brown eyes and smiled softly at her. She stuttered a little, feeling embarrassed by her attraction to him as if it were something visible and obvious. She followed his gesture near the room's entrance and took notice of a notebook sitting on a desk to the left of the doors. A few of the other students were gathered around waiting to sign their names in the notebook. The sign above the table said *please sign in.*

"Sorry, I didn't see that. I'm going to get in line right now", she said as she stood and rushed off to join the group of her peers. As she waited to sign her name on the sheet, she wondered if the guy she had just spoken to was the professor. After pondering the thought for a moment, she decided that it was probably very unlikely because of how young he appeared to be. As soon as she had settled back into her seat and got ready for class to begin, a balding man with a beard in his late-forties, or early-fifties walked to the front of the room and to a podium. This guy looked much more like what she imagined her professor would. He introduced himself as Professor Wilson and started straight into the lecture after asking his assistant, Brennon, who had reminded Ella to sign in earlier, to pass out the class syllabus. Ella watched Brennon closely as he walked from table to table, sitting a small stack of papers on each one and telling the student on the end to take one and pass the rest down the row. Brennon smiled at her again as he walked by and her heart pounded in her chest with excitement. It seemed like it could have been a flirty smile. After that she was unable to get him out of her mind. A warm tingle and the wetness in her panties became an all-day distraction for her. The unwelcome distraction would continue returning every time she saw or even thought of him over the next few days. This guy had Ella more worked up than she had ever felt before.

She was laying on her twin-sized bed, with purple comforters in the mostly empty, and unusually undecorated dorm room that she shared with a girl named Fallon. Fallon was out, as she often was, so Ella was using the private time to do the only thing she could think to do to get the thoughts of Brennon to stop being so obtrusive and terribly distracting. Hopefully this release would make it so that she could focus on completing the introduction essay for her English class, which was due soon. She fantasized of him kissing her and touching her all over her body. Her thoughts were racing through her mind as she fiercely rubbed her wet pussy. She focused on trying to pretend it was his hand in her panties instead of her own. She began growing frustrated, as the rush did not come as fast as it once had, that was probably due to the change in how often she had been needing to do this. She rubbed faster, keeping the usually effective circular motion, circling around her clit. Finally, her body tensed up and she moaned in unbelievable pleasure, finally relieving her pent-up sexual frustrations.

Her body went limp for just a moment, and she took a deep breath before reaching over to the table beside her bed and grabbing her laptop from it. She put her hand into her panties to see how much cum was there. She pulled her hand up to her face to look. When she did, she licked her finger, tasting her own sweet nectar. Suddenly the door swung open. Ella opened the laptop quickly and sat it on her lap in a single motion and got back to working on her essay. Her roommate, Fallon, had just walked in and immediately began undressing herself in front of Ella. Ella noticed her perfect body; her dark hair fell back down to her hips as she pulled her top over her head. Ella looked away quickly so her roommate would not catch her looking at her. Fallon glanced over at Ella, with a curious expression while Ella pretended to be captivated with typing on her laptop.

"I know we haven't hung out much yet, but do you want to come out to a party with me tonight?", Fallon asked unexpectedly. She eyed Ella with a look of sympathy. It was probably due to the fact that Ella had barely left this room since her arrival to college, other than to go to her classes of course, and she had been thinking about how badly she needed some time out. So, she agreed to go out despite how nervous she felt about the idea. Just moments later, when Ella announced that she was ready, Fallon looked her over and crossed her arms with a thinking expression on her face. Ella looked down at herself questioningly after noticing the stunning blue shimmering dress Fallon was wearing. It was accompanied by an adorable white half jacket and black pumps. Fallon looked stunning, and Ella felt out of place next to her.

"You can borrow something of mine", Fallon said suggestively as she turned towards her closet. She glanced through her clothes for a minute or two and then pulled out a short maroon dress and tossed it at Ella with a smile. "Can you wear a size four?", she asked.

"Yes", Ella answered as she eyed the dress in her hands. She obediently stepped out of the comfort of her blue jeans and floral cowl-neck blouse, which was probably the most party-appropriate thing she currently owned, and she stepped into the dress. The thick knitted material clung tightly to her body as she pulled it up. She was surprised to see it looked great and accentuated her curves quite nicely. The sleeves wrapped around her arms hanging over her shoulders leaving her neck and the top of her chest exposed. After asking her shoe-size, Fallon handed Ella some black boots with short heels. Ella slipped those on as well and was surprised by how comfortable they were.

"One last thing", Fallon said, slowly dragging out the words as she rooted around in her bag. Her hand emerged with a tube of lipstick. She uncapped it and carefully applied it to Ella's full lips, then she looked at Ella with a smile, clearly satisfied with her work.

"Am I ready?", Ella asked eagerly. Fallon nodded with a grin. Ella looked back at herself in the full-length mirror that hung on the inside of their dorm room's door and her big brown eyes widened in surprise. She could not believe she was looking at herself right now, she felt a wave of new confidence as she took in her much-changed reflection. The dress's off the shoulder sleeves made her small bust appear to be much larger, the dress highlighted her thin waist and showed off her thick butt and thighs. Even she could not deny that she looked stunning, but it still did not stop her from feeling incredibly nervous about going to her first college party. When they walked into the party, Ella had her arms crossed tightly over her chest and holding each other as if she were cold, but it was not the September chill that was making her cross her arms. She felt very exposed in front of all these people with this tiny dress on. Fallon apparently saw what was going on, she leaned over close to Ella and told her to relax and breathe. She promised Ella that there was nothing to worry about.

"Why don't you have a drink", she suggested. Ella looked back at her and nodded.

"Yeah, that will help", Ella decided.

So, Ella forced her arms down to her sides, stood up straight, and walked over to the drink table as confidently as she could. There was a mountain of solo cups and a few coolers with spouts on the table where people lined up to fill their cups with whatever was in those coolers. Before she could even make her way through the dense crowd to get a solo cup, one was already being passed in her direction. She knew better than to accept a drink from just anyone. She had heard about the dangers of accepting drinks from strangers her entire life.

"No tha- ", she started to say but she stopped without even finishing her word, once she looked up at the person who was passing the cup to her, which was full of some blue drink. She smiled, took it from his hand and took a big gulp of the sugary blue liquid. The innocent-looking drink was burning as it made its way down her throat. "Thank you", she managed to say through the fire in her chest. Brennon smiled at her knowingly, but he was polite enough to not mention her obvious unfamiliarity with her surroundings.

"I never imagined that college parties would be your thing", he said with a slight slur in his deep sexy voice.

"Well, I don't really know if it is my 'thing' or not yet", she said truthfully, but with as much confidence as she could muster up, "It's my first time attending one", she finished.

"Well, I think a tour is in order m'lady", he said gesturing dramatically past the crowded table that held the coolers and mountain of solo cups. She giggled at his silliness and walked ahead of him. They made their way down a hallway and they talked as he showed her each room of the house, which she learned was a historic building. He informed her that the house was owned by the school. He said students often used it for parties, even though it was not technically allowed, but most of the school's staff was well-aware of the shenanigans that went on here. They ignored it because they had done the same when they were young and in college. As Ella listened, she was starting to feel the warm and tingly effects of the alcohol just a few minutes after finishing her drink. She liked how good it made her feel. She had sipped her parents wine a few times on special occasions, but she had never felt what it was like to be drunk before.

She was enjoying the boost of confidence and the much-needed courage it was kindly lending her. The pair sat down beside one another on a bench, in a seemingly unused office that was on the far end of the hallway, and away from the crowd. It was either the alcohol, or just being alone with him that immediately got her pussy wetter than she had ever been before. She decided it was probably a mix of the two. While he was telling a story about his own first time at a college party, she was staring at him thinking about the naughty things she wanted him to do to her. She had hardly been paying attention to what he was saying because she was too busy imagining his hands exploring her body.

He glanced in her direction, and she looked back at him dreamily wondering if he could see it in her eyes how badly she was wanting him right now. She suddenly wondered why he continued looking at her expectantly, she had not heard much of what he was saying through her fantasizing about him. She began to hope he had not asked a question and was now waiting for her response, but then he put his hand on her thigh. She held her breath, and her chest pounded in anticipation as he slowly trailed his fingers lightly up her thigh, and closer to the place that was now tingling so intensely she had to fight the urge to squirm beside him. Then in one swift motion he moved his hands and firmly gripped the backs of her thighs, and lifted her up with ease, holding her against himself. He carried her forward until her back was pressed against the wall with his weight pressed against her. She could feel his hard cock pressed against her as well, which made her head begin to swim, and earned him a moan.

She noticed how dizzy she was feeling and wondered how much of it was the alcohol she had drank and how much of it was his intoxicating presence. She began to consider the possibility that they might end up having sex if things continued on their current trajectory. For the moment, she was still a virgin, which she felt immensely embarrassed about considering she was in college, her nerves began to take hold, making her doubtful that she was making the right choice. She wanted him badly though, and it wasn't even just her that wanted him, her body wanted him, every cell was pushing her to give in to her desires. She could taste the sweet drink he had just been sipping on as they kissed. He squeezed her ass, and trailed kisses up to her ear. He pulled her earlobe into his mouth nibbling on it gently. She felt his breath on her ear.

"Tell me how badly you want my hard cock", he whispered into her ear. Her heart began to race as she tried to make the words come out. At first, she only let out a moan but then as if it were a miracle, the words came out of her mouth naturally and seductively.

"Oh Brennon, I want your cock so bad", she cried out. "My pussy is wet and ready for it", She said breathlessly. She wondered where that had come from. She felt surprisingly proud of herself for sounding so seductive and sexy.

"Mmmm, yeah baby", Brennon said back to her, letting her know that she had given him exactly what he had asked for. He lightly bit and sucked on her neck for a moment and she moaned in response. It was clear what was about to happen. Ella pondered whether she should tell him about her being a virgin, or if it would just ruin the moment. Before, she could process her thoughts or come to any conclusions, the door swung open and they both startled a little at the sound.

"Well, that did not take long!", Fallon exclaimed, rushing heatedly into the room.

Ella straightened her legs, and her feet touched the floor as Brennon released his grip on her thighs with a confused look that quickly turned to guilt when he saw and recognized Fallon. Fallon grabbed Ella by the arm. Ella was stunned into silence, so she let Fallon guide her from the room feeling conflicted and confused. When Brennon was out of sight Ella's heart dropped into her stomach. She felt painful disappointment and unfulfilled desire. As they walked back to their dorm room Fallon apologized for her intrusion. She explained that she had only been trying to look out for Ella.

"It's just, you seem like you're way too sweet a person to be taken advantage of the way he does with girls", she started. "I mean, from what I hear around campus, he does this all the time."

"Really?", Ella said looking confused.

Fallon told Ella of her own experience with Brennon she had over the summer, when she had been here for her orientation, which was just a few weeks before school had started. She decided to go check out one of the parties because that is the part of college everyone talks the most about, so she snuck out of the hotel she was staying at and crashed a party. Brennon was the first person she met who had spoken to her while she was at the wild event. They started talking and she got the impression that he was really into her, and she liked him too. So, when he made a move, she did not object to it.

Ella felt a pang of jealousy when Fallon revealed that she had let Brennon fuck her, but apparently, the next day Fallon had looked around hoping to exchange phone numbers with Brennon, and she did not see him anywhere. Fallon had been disappointed, but she figured she would catch up with him when school started. On her first day she talked to some people about him and apparently, he got around like that quite a bit. When she finally saw him again, on the first day of English class, he acted as if he had never seen her before.

"He's hardly made eye contact with me since then", she told Ella, "I feel really used", she finished.

After she was done telling her story, Ella comforted Fallon. As she hugged Fallon, she felt a sore spot on her neck. Ella rubbed the spot for a moment trying to figure out what it was until it caught Fallon's attention.

"Did he leave a hickey on your neck?" Fallon asked with an offended look.

"I…I guess so", Ella said remembering how amazing his mouth felt against her neck. Ella could not help it, she honestly still wanted Brennon just as badly as she had before. The desire she had for him remained completely unaffected by the knowledge gained from Fallon's story. It was not that Ella did not believe Fallon; it was just that she was perfectly willing to accept the risk. She tried, for the sake of Fallon's feelings to convince herself that it was inevitably a bad idea to get involved with someone who had a reputation like that. Ella desperately wanted to put a stop to whatever was going on between them. Ella really did not want to betray Fallon's friendship, especially after she had been so nice. Fallon told Ella that she would not be upset with her if she still wanted to see where it goes with him, but Ella could hear the hurt in Fallon's voice as she said it. Ella felt nearly obligated to not get intimate with him. Unfortunately, her mind kept almost involuntarily trying to think of ways that she could get alone with him again so they could finish what they had started in that office. It left a raging war between hormones and wanting to be a loyal friend to Fallon. Ella knew the temptation could easily become too much, especially if Brennon were to actively pursue her.

Ella walked into the English classroom with her head down as her heart pounded in her chest. She immediately saw Brennon standing at the front of the room sorting through some papers at the professor's podium, looking as sexy as ever. She noticed how cute the jeans he had on made his butt look. When he was finished with the papers, he set them aside in a neat stack further down on the nearby desk. He briefly looked up from what he was doing and gazed directly at the place where Ella sat each day. They made brief eye contact before they both looked away nervous and wondering what the other was thinking. Ella tried to keep her eyes down and away from him during class and to pay him no attention. After class she quickly tucked her book under her arm and began to make her escape from the class, with her heart still thumping hard in her chest. She made it about halfway down the hall that turned towards her next class when she heard his voice calling her name loudly behind her.

"Hey, I was hoping to talk to you", he smiled nervously as he fiddled with some keys in his hands, "sorry about the other night", he added. Ella quickly assured him that he had done nothing that she did not want him to do. He looked relieved and he asked when her next class was beginning, he glanced over her body and silently wondered why she hid her stunning figure behind the baggy clothes she usually wore. She glanced up at the clock that was hanging on the wall above a classroom door. She felt disappointment when she had to tell him she only had 20 minutes to spare before she had a lab.

"Would you mind if I walked with you?", he asked hopefully.

"No, of course not", Ella said smiling. She noticed some people staring at them as they walked down the hall, and she wondered if it was a normal thing for him to be walking through the halls with a girl by his side. After walking down, a flight of stairs and a long hallway, they stopped in front of Ella's biology lab and she suddenly decided that now was as good a time as any to tell him about her still in-tact virginity. She wanted to go ahead and rip off the Band-Aid and get it over with.

"So, I probably need to tell you something.", Ella began, "I only have a few minutes, but I want to go ahead and get this out in the open".

"Okay", Brennon said with an apprehensive smile. She blurted it out plainly, and without any further explanations. He immediately looked downward and she could tell he felt bad about being so forward with her the other night.

"I'm sorry I had no idea", he said. Ella was quick to remind him that she wanted what had happened at the party and she assured him that it was nothing he should feel bad about. She said she had wished Fallon had not stormed in like that and dragged her away.

"Yeah, I may have upset her a little", he started to explain. Ella stopped him and told him she was already made aware of what happened between the two of them, and she told him that it had no effect on her feelings towards him. He looked relieved again and she wondered if he might actually want to fuck her as badly as she had been wanting him. Brennon broke the silence that had settled between them to ask Ella if she wanted to hang out with him again soon, he had a suggestive look on his face, and she knew right away what he meant.

"Of course, I would", Ella said as she leaned in to hug him tight. He ran his hand over her ass as he hugged her back and she giggled. After that they said bye to each other for now and Ella walked reluctantly into her lab and took her seat.

Once Ella's lab was finished, she went and got something quick to eat from the dining hall, and then she walked back to her dorm room. By the time she made it back, she felt completely exhausted by the day's exciting events and she plopped down onto her bed adjusting her pillow behind the arch of her back. She wanted to be upfront and honest, and tell Fallon about what happened today, but she had not made it back to the dorm yet, so Ella got out her laptop to bide the time. She decided to sign into the online portal for her English class so she could submit the assignment she had finished last night. When she tried to log in, a box popped up, *Login attempt failed*, it said. She tried again using the exact same password she had been given by Professor Wilson and it failed again. This time she slowed herself down and carefully typed the password, paying attention to the paper that she received with the class syllabus. It had her login information on it, so she was certain it was entered correctly this time. She hit enter again and right as she did, it dawned on her that she had already changed it to a more personal password. She tried to log in again with her own password, but unfortunately, she had already made too many login attempts and was now locked out of the account.

She cussed under her breath, and she came to the conclusion that there probably was nothing she could do until tomorrow, so Ella finished other class work and when Fallon still had not shown up, she gave up and pulled her comforter over her shoulders and went to sleep. Ella woke up earlier than usual and used the extra time to take a long shower and do a little bit of her seemingly endless schoolwork. Fallon invited Ella to have breakfast with some of her friends, but she needed some time to herself, so she politely declined the offer, and soon after, Fallon rushed out of the dorm complaining about being late. Ella noticed she had left her lipstick on her side table along with a few other things she usually took along with her. Ella thought about the other night, and how nice the lipstick had looked on her. She did not think that Fallon would mind too much if she used it, so she took it off the table, put some on, and put it back where it had been found. Ella smiled into the mirror and studied the effect it had on her pale complexion. After looking herself up and down once more Ella put her books in her bag and left the dorm feeling antsy and excited because she knew she had English today, meaning she would get to see him again.

Ella got to her class, and they jumped right into the lecture as usual. Halfway through the class professor Wilson finished the lesson they had been working on and called for the class to take a short recess so he could get himself prepared for his next lecture. Ella took the opportunity to request help with her account. She quietly approached his desk and when he glanced at her, she asked him what she should do about her account being locked. Without ever looking up from his computer, he told her that Brennon would have to help get it sorted out because his day was fully booked. Then he asked if she was available after class to meet with Brennon so he could get her logged into her account. Luckily, she had over two hours before her next class began because there was no biology lab today, so she happily told him that she had time.

"I will talk to Brennon and see if he has time after class as well", he said hurriedly. She thanked Professor Wilson and went back to her desk and sat down. She flipped through her book as she waited for class to resume. Not long after the professor resumed his lecture on how to correctly format citations for different writing styles, Brennon walked over to Ella's desk, and stuck a blue sticky note on it. As he walked away, she quickly grabbed it before anyone else could see what it said just in case it was personal. She held it under the desk and looked at it in secret. There were just four words, *see you after class* it simply stated in his neat, curvy handwriting. It had a little winking smiley face at the bottom. Ella looked up and smiled at Brennon to let him know that she was excited to see him. The remaining forty-five minutes of the class, Ella was very distracted by an intense giddy feeling in her stomach as several scenarios played out in her head that almost always ended in the two of them completely naked and exploring each other's bodies.

She knew that this was very unlikely to happen after class today, especially considering the professor would probably still be here to supervise them. After class, Ella stayed behind as the other students rushed on to their next class. Brennon came over and sat at the desk beside her and opened his laptop appearing to be all-business today. He said nothing about the sexual tension that lingered thick in the air between them. He quickly got Ella a new temporary password, and he asked her to sign in just to make sure it worked. While she was signing in, she noticed Mr. Wilson leaving the room with his bag over his shoulder. Ella successfully signed into the English portal.

"Thank you", she said smiling at him expectantly.

"How much more time do you have?", he asked plainly with a serious look on his face.

When she told him she still had over an hour to spare, he got up, without uttering a word, and locked the classroom doors. He turned and looked at her hungrily. He smiled mischievously at her and winked. Her body responded to the gesture immediately. He walked over to her looking confident and sexy. She was nervous about being caught until he assured her it was okay which made her immediately relax. He told her that Mr. Wilson would be gone the rest of the day, and other than the dean, who was too busy to worry about two students being alone in a classroom, no one else had a key. Ella bit her bottom lip feeling excited and ready. Brennon leaned in close to kiss her. Their lips met as he lifted her up the same way he had at the party, except this time he laid her across the professor's desk. Ella held her breath and her chest pounded with excitement as he slowly unbuttoned her shirt, each button exposing more of her bare skin when released. When he made it to the last one, he started leaving a trail of kisses up her stomach until he reached the band of her purple bra.

She arched her back instinctively as he reached under her and swiftly unclasped the bra. She slipped it over her arms and dropped it to the floor. She trembled as Brennon cupped her little breasts with his hands and he leaned in to take one of her nipples into his mouth. He sucked hard on the tiny nipple, and it perked up immediately in response. Ella moaned in anticipation as his hands reached down to the button of her jeans. He quickly unbuttoned them and pulled the tight material down her hips, kissing her trembling skin all the way down. She watched him as he methodically removed her shoes and socks, one at a time, and then pulled her jeans over her ankles and completely off. Then he pushed her panties to the side and stuck his fingers into her tight, wet pussy.

"Ready?", He asked, looking at her sweetly.

"Yes", she breathed, it was hardly even a sound, just her mouth making the shape of the word she meant to say.

He took his thick, hard cock out of his pants and held it in his hand. He grabbed her hand and put it on his boner. As she touched it, she felt intimidated by its size. The intimidating feelings were forgotten when he started rubbing her clit with the head of his big cock. She felt like she could cum for him at any moment, but she held it back, wanting to take it slow and enjoy every moment and store it into her memory forever. He grabbed her hips and easily turned her over onto her hands and knees, so she was facing away from him. He rubbed his cock in the wetness from her excitement, and then she felt the pressure of it trying to enter her tight pussy. She gasped and squealed as he pushed into her pussy.

"Fucking hell, it's so tight", he grunted, trying to find a good position. She felt a dull pain in her lower stomach that lasted only a moment, but it did not matter to her because the pleasure of feeling his cock inside of her greatly outweighed the momentary pain by a long shot.

He thrust gently and slowly into her at first. He noticed his cock tinged with the blood from breaking her hymen. She pushed her hips back against his cock, so he started increasing the speed and began to thrust into her with more voice. Her tight pussy felt so good as it squeezed his cock. He took her by her hips and started fucking her hard, making sure he hit her cervix. He did this three times in a row before he found a way into her that made her gasp for breath. He pulled her head back by her hair, so she was staring straight up at the ceiling and he put his cock deep into her pussy. He fucked her hard as her tits bounced, he stroked her cunt with his cock and she almost came again when he pulled her down on her knees.

She started stroking his cock with her hand. He pulled her lips down onto his cock, and he groaned as he came inside her mouth. It was even more intense than he had imagined. It seemed like he was coming every time he pulled her head closer to his cock. He grabbed her head, and he made her lick his cock clean. She sucked hard on his cock and she felt it swell and he groaned loudly, pushing her head down. Her tongue was covered in his cum as she stroked his cock with her hand. She licked and sucked, every last drop of cum she could get. He pulled her up and held her. Her body was covered in sweat, but she felt exhilarated. She knew she could get used to this.

They created a makeshift bed with some things lying around in the classroom and they lay there relaxing, Ella was stroking his cock, trying not to let it go limp. She looked into his eyes and they both had a silent conversation between them. They both knew what they wanted to do to each other, but neither one wanted to push the other one into doing it. They knew the other would probably back out. They talked about their past relationships and other things as they both worked their fingers slowly in and out of each other's mouth.

They both knew what was going to happen next and they both wanted it. They opened their eyes and saw that the time had come to share. They looked at each other in amazement. "Are you sure about this?", he asked, still holding her hand.

"Yes, but what about you?", she asked, also still holding his hand.

"I am sure. I want this too."

Ella lifted her leg and slipped off the desk. She got on all fours and let him slide his cock inside her. She wrapped her arms around his back and buried her head in his shoulder. He grabbed her ass cheeks and slid his cock in and out of her pussy.

"Fuck, your pussy feels incredible.", he groaned

"I want you inside me," Ella whispered in his ear. She got on all fours again. He slid his cock in slowly at first, until he was deep inside her. He started fucking her slow, making sure he felt every inch of her tight pussy. He pulled her hair as he fucked her slowly, then started fucking her faster. He grabbed her hips and started to slam his cock in her with a force she didn't think she could take. Ella could not believe the way his cock was fucking her. He kept fucking her harder and faster, as her ass was bouncing up and down. He suddenly realized he was about to come, so he pulled out, not wanting to risk getting her pregnant. He groaned as he watched his cum shoot out all over her lower back and on her beautiful ass. Ella rolled to her side, looking up at him. Brennon told her to stay still, and that he would be right back as he stepped into the professor's office and wet some tissue with a water bottle. She remained laying on her side until he returned and cleaned the mess of cum and blood off her. She turned and hopped off the desk as he wiped himself off. She smiled shyly and hoped they would be able to do that again.

Dayna listened quietly to Ella's entire story intently and wished her first time had been as steamy as Ella's had been.

"That was really hot", Dayna said as she dramatically fanned her face with her hand. Ella was feeling pretty buzzed from the martinis, and she realized she had not eaten much that day, so she placed an order for a few appetizers for them to share. "I honestly always figured you'd be pretty basic as an adult", Dayna told her,

"My parents tried to raise me to be conservative, but I had to learn to have fun at some point" Ella responded with a thoughtful expression, "Brennon definitely helped me start to do that". She explained that she and Brennon had dated for a couple months after that, they got along well together, but neither of them was ready to be in a serious relationship, they were far too busy enjoying college, so they decided to go their separate ways, and remain on good terms, although after leaving the school, they only contacted one another every now and then. "He gave me a great first sexual experience though," Ella said, smirking.

"I can only think of one thing that could possibly have made it better", Dayna teased. Her short hair bounced around as she bawled her hand into a fist and moved it side by side near her cheek as she pushed her other cheek out with her tongue, a gesture that indicated she meant a blowjob. Both women laughed loudly, and several people turned to give them an annoyed glance, but the ladies hardly noticed.

Ella rolled her eyes, "Sure that's fun but I much prefer being on the receiving end of that".

"Why choose when you can do both?", Dayna asked jokingly and they both burst into a fit of laughter. "That reminds me of something fun I did once", Dayna remarked.

"Well, it is your turn to be the storyteller", Ella leaned forward patiently waiting for Dayna to start telling her story.

Dayna's Satisfying Deal (69)

Dayna had not really been paying attention as Jean, the property manager who was an older red-haired woman, and spoke in an obnoxiously loud voice, gave her a tour of the small, basic two-bedroom house. Dayna was already on borrowed time living with her mom and her mom's boyfriend, her boyfriend was a pervert and she managed to make him angry every time he made a pass at her. Her mom would ask her to keep the peace, but she could not. So even her mom was a little ready for her to get her own place, and she knew this place was it unless she wanted to experience what being homeless is like. The thought made her shudder, so she pretended to be interested and after the showing she indicated that she was happy with everything and ready to sign the lease and pay the deposit. The maintenance man walked in the house right as Jean had pulled the lease from the back of her stack of papers. The maintenance man eyed Dayna as he began doing a final check of the house. He was in his late twenties, maybe early thirties. He was surprisingly good looking, very fit from his physically demanding job, he looked a little rough around the edges in a way which Dayna could not decide if she found sexy or not.

She straightened her legs and bent over the counter to sign the lease; she took special care to arch her ass out as far as possible just to see if the maintenance man took notice of her. He took the bait, Dayna watched him almost run smack into the wall as he tried to gawk at her perky ass as she bent seductively over the kitchen counter.

"Are you about done in here Greg?", Jean yelled, also taking notice of the maintenance man, whose name was apparently Greg, and his less than focused work ethic. Jean made her way up the hill to get a camera and a few other things she needed. Greg angrily muttered something under his breath before he disappeared to the back of the house. Dayna held in a giggle as she watched the scene play out. Once Jean was gone, she continued signing the last pages when suddenly she felt something behind her. She jumped and turned to see Gregg.

"You shouldn't fuck with people like that, little slut", he said. Dayna just laughed as he pressed his weight against her body, pinning her to the counter. He backs up and returns to work without another word as Jean walks back inside. Dayna gave the papers back to Jean along with Jean's pen and all the cash for the deposit and first month's rent. Jean counted the money once out loud so Dayna could hear and a second time to herself. Then she shoved it all into a large black zipper pouch greedily. She tucked the pouch protectively in a fanny pack she had been wearing, which was buckled firmly around her wide hips.

"When can I start moving in?", Dayna asked, trying to avoid showing how desperate and eager she was. After talking to Greg for a moment, Jean informed Dayna that she would have to wait until Monday to move in because the air conditioner needed a replacement part that could not be bought until the heat and air store opens on Monday.

Dayna got in her car and drove home as she chanted "just 2 more days", over and over in her head. She hated it there, her mom's boyfriend was an ass, and he was constantly trying to hit on Dayna. He was a creep, and she could not wait to get out of that disgusting broken down hellhole she called home, although she felt terrible about leaving her mom alone with him. After pulling into her mom's driveway, she sat in the car for a while, listening to the radio and thinking about the furniture she wants to get for her new place. She looked at the clock on her car radio and realized it was almost eleven, "Hopefully Danny will be passed out drunk by now", she thought as she gathered her things to go inside.

She opened the car door and got out, carefully closing it behind her. She crept slowly up the steps skipping the ones she knew were loud. She carefully unlocked the door and turned the doorknob slowly. She crept inside quietly. Danny appeared to be asleep on the couch, she breathed a sigh of relief and began to tiptoe past him to get to her room.

"You find a place yet?", he suddenly said.

Dayna jumped at the abrupt disruption and sighed loudly. "I will be out of here Monday, Danny now leaves me alone please, I'm going to my room.", she barked angrily.

"Sure, you don't want daddy to come tuck you in and kiss you goodnight?", Danny said, showing off his rotting teeth as he smiled.

"Ew, no thanks", she responded feeling disgusted.

"Stupid bitch", she heard him say as she made her way quickly to her room and shut the door.

She locked the door behind her and got straight into bed, her insomnia kept her up for a few hours as she stared at the alarm clock on her nightstand beside her bed. She woke up around ten in the morning and began packing her things into boxes, while she remained locked in her room. Her mom always worked long hours on weekends, so she avoided leaving her room because she did not like being around Danny when her mom was not there. She carefully and neatly packed everything over the next couple days, staying in her room, only coming out to jot to the bathroom across the hall. By Monday she had her whole room cleaned spotless too. She felt her stomach growl. She had gone two days surviving off a box of Fig Newtons, a Moon Pie, and a couple bottles of Gatorade she had stashed in her room. She decided her mom was probably home by now, so she left her room to find herself something to eat for breakfast.

When she opened her bedroom door, she immediately smelled a delicious and unfamiliar smell that made her stomach growl and lurch even more than it already had been. She walked into the kitchen and was shocked to see her mom making a big breakfast. There was fried bologna, pancakes, and potatoes, which sat on separate plates beside the stove as her mom scrambled eggs in a buttered pan and biscuits baked in the oven.

"Hey baby girl", her mom said as Dayna sat down at the table, "Danny said you're leaving today, and I thought I'd make you a farewell breakfast".

"Thanks mom", Dayna said looking around "Where is Danny anyway?", she asked.

"Oh, he went to help his brother with something.", she replied. Dayna was glad to get to spend some alone time with her mom before she had to leave. They sat at the table and ate breakfast together for the first time in forever and Dayna told her mom all about her new place.

After they had eaten her mom pulled out an envelope from her purse and held it out to Dayna. "I got you a housewarming gift", she said, giving her the envelope, "Please don't tell Danny", she said putting her finger over her lips, to signal that it was a secret.

Dayna carefully opened the envelope and took out a card decorated with a floral pattern. Something fell out of the envelope and into her lap as she opened it. She saw that "I love you, from mom" was written on the inside of the card as she picked up the thing that fell from the inside. After examining it she realized it was a furniture gift card for one hundred dollars. She thanked her mom and hugged her tight, before tucking the gift card into her pocket. Her mom had also packed a few boxes with some of the extra dishes and towels she had. Afterwards, Dayna packed as much as she could into her car and headed to her new place.

When she pulled into the gravel driveway, Greg, the maintenance man, had just been locking the door and leaving her house. He most likely just finished fixing the air conditioner. He handed her the keys, as he looked her up and down. She took the keys from his hand and thanked him before heading inside. She opened the door and brought the things she had packed in her car into the house and sat them on the floor. As she did, Greg stared intently, enjoying the view of her ass each time she bent over. She turned to shut the door and caught Greg once again eying her and she smiled and waved as he got into his old truck. As she looked at the way he carried himself as if he did not have a care in the world, she decided that she did find him quite attractive. He may not be the best-looking guy she had ever been into, but he had a way about him that made her think he would be good in bed. She wondered what fucking him would be like. She imagined his cock was probably big just based on the size and shape of his body.

She still had a bunch of stuff she needed to get from her room, and she wanted to get it done before Danny got the chance to go through it and confiscate anything he might want. She shivered at the thought of him going through and touching all her things. She pulled her phone out of her back pocket and began scrolling through her contacts trying to think of who might have a truck. After calling 8 people, only half of whom had a truck, she was still no closer to getting her things from her mom's house. Her uncle Rich was currently out of town for a job and everyone else was busy with work or family or had already left for college. Despite getting accepted into a decent school, Dayna decided to skip college. It is so expensive, and she would prefer to go ahead and enter the workforce, because she knew she would have to keep at least 2 jobs to afford school and trying to juggle that with going to school seemed like too much. She also really needed the break from school honestly.

Her mind went back to thinking about Greg, she thought about how sexy he looked getting into that old truck, his muscles expanding anytime he would tense up his body, which happened quite a bit when he was working. She looked up and her eyes widened as an idea came to mind. She remembered that Jean had said his phone number had been written on the lease just in case emergency maintenance is ever needed. She pulled out her copy of the lease and began flipping through the pages, scanning them fiercely. Once she found the number she was looking for, she punched it into her phone. She hesitated for just a moment and then dialed it and listened as it began to ring.

"Who's this?" He said with a clipped tone that indicated he was annoyed by the call.

"Hi, this is Dayna, from the house on...", she began.

"I know which one", he said, cutting her words short as his tone went from annoyed to amused.

"Sorry to bother you", she began, "But I noticed you have a truck, and see, I'm trying to figure out a way to get the rest of my stuff from my old place." Greg listened patiently on the other end as Dayna rambled on about how far it was and that it would only take a single trip, and that she was willing to pay him, and how she could not afford much and that she could not think of anyone else to ask. Dayna was not great at asking for help, she liked to see herself as an independent person and often refused to ask for help because most of the few people she has accepted help from have tried to hold it over her head or use it against her in some way, but she really wanted her belongings safely here with her, so she was willing to accept the risk. So many of those things are special to her, they remind her of the good memories she had of her childhood. All the notes she and Ella used to write to each other and pass in between classes, what she had left of her grandmother's jewelry, and the only photo she has of her dad is all packed up in those boxes. Greg did not give her an answer, all he would say was that he would come by to see if they could work out a deal. Dayna was determined that she would work out a deal with him.

"Luckily mom has the day off work, so that should keep him out of my stuff for now", she thought feeling a little relieved by the realization, "but I've got to be there to get everything first thing in the morning because once she leaves for work, it probably won't take him long to start going through it all, especially since it's all packed up in one place and not hidden all over the room like I had it when that was my room".

Dayna had begun unpacking the little bit of stuff she did have here in her house. She blew up a twin-size air mattress with the little electric pump it came with and placed it on the floor of the biggest of the two bedrooms. She threw a sheet over the air mattress and topped that with her pillow and a fleece blanket with a blue snowflake pattern that she had got for Christmas last year. In the kitchen, she organized the cabinets and refrigerator with the dishes and a few days' worth of groceries that her mom had packed. and she stacked the towels and washcloths in the bathroom closet after placing her toothbrush and other toiletries on the sink. She looked around her empty place and she decided she would try to go to the furniture store tomorrow and see if they delivered, the place being so empty made her feel even more lonely than she already did. Then she heard a low rumble that kept getting closer coming from outside her place.

"That's probably Greg pulling up in the driveway", she thought excitedly, ready to get away from the nagging feeling of worry and loneliness that plagued her every moment she spent in this barren house. She met him at the door, already holding it open gesturing for him to come inside. He smiled at her flirtatiously as he walked in, he looked around at the place and asked her what she had in mind. She told him again that she did not think it would take more than a single load because she only had one small bedroom to get stuff from. She pulled a small wad of money from her pocket and he smiled, looking at her with an amused expression that was almost condescending. She counted out twenty-seven dollars and smiled at him as she told him that was all she had.

"Where's your folk's place?", he asked, putting his hands in the pockets of his ragged and stained blue jeans. She told them it was about 35 minutes East and he burst out laughing in response, "Do you know how much it costs in gas alone to run that beast out there?". She nodded her head as a look of disappointment crossed her face. "I will make you a deal though. Anyway, I don't really want your money", he added. She had a feeling that she was not going to like the deal he was about to offer, but curiosity and sheer determination made her ask regardless.

"What do you want?", she said quietly as her shoulders slumped.

"I want that thing you were trying to show off to me the other day", he plainly stated with a devilish smile. She looked back at him unsure of exactly what he was referring to, and too nervous to say anything. "I want that ass", he said more directly this time.

"I'm not going to fuck you for a ride to get my stuff", she said looking very offended. "I'm not a hooker!", she exclaimed as her face began to flush with a mix of anger and embarrassment.

He started waving his hands around, "woah, woah, woah, slow down their girl", he said authoritatively, "First off I did not say anything about fucking you", he clarified, "and I have friends who are working girls, and I have incredible respect for them, so don't you be insulting them".

Dayna instinctively apologized for offending Greg although she could not tell how serious he was. She asked him to clarify exactly what it is that he was wanting from her if he did not want to fuck her. He explained that he loved eating pussy, and ass too, and he might like to get a little bit of head as well.

"And you should watch how you judge them girls, they aren't doing anything besides being strong enough to take control of their lives and being quite resourceful too", he suggested. Dayna saw his point when he explained it that way. She carefully considered his offer and the fact that she had already been thinking about fucking Greg, and she felt a little less ashamed to accept his offer after hearing what he had to say on the matter which she also considered may have been his motive. Dayna hesitated for a moment before determination pushed her into accepting his offer. Then she asked him if he was able to be here tomorrow morning to go get her stuff from her parents before she completed her end of the deal, she told him it was because she wanted to have someplace comfortable to complete her end of the agreement.

"Alright, that's fine with me, but you better make good on your end of the bargain because I can make your life very difficult here if you don't, I could probably even get you tossed out of here if I wanted", he gave her a look that indicated that he was serious about the matter. She assured him that she would hold up her end of the bargain. She asked if he could come around six in the morning and he said that was fine. He was normally up at five anyway. Before heading out the door and to his truck, he politely wished her a good night.

Her thoughts raced through her mind as she pondered what had just happened between her and Greg and how apprehensive and confused, she felt about the agreement as she began getting herself ready for bed. She thought about when she was younger, in the weeks right before her mom had met Danny, and how they stayed in different hotel rooms, moving every few days, sometimes only staying in a place for a single night. She remembered frequently seeing women of all ages, mostly dressed in short dresses, and skirts all around the hotels, her mom had once referred to them as hookers, it was years before she understood what that meant. She thought about what Greg said, and it made sense. She went to bed thinking about those women and the new-found respect she had for them. She was startled awake to a bang on her front door. She looked around confused momentarily and almost immediately realized what was going on. She could not believe she had forgot to set an alarm. "Fuck", she said as she jumped up and ran to the door to meet Greg.

"Good morning sunshine", he said sarcastically, "you ready?". She asked him to wait just a moment and assured him it would not take her long to get ready. She ran straight to the restroom without waiting for an answer, and then she brushed her teeth, quickly applied some deodorant, and threw her hair up in a ponytail. She ran back to the door, stopping to grab her purse along the way. She slammed the door and locked it behind her. Greg was already sitting in the truck waiting patiently, and typing on his phone, he kept looking down at her shirt with a smile on his face. She followed his gaze and realized she had been in such a rush she had forgot to put a bra on. Her puckered nipples poked through her shirt and it was clearly visible. She smiled back at Greg and shrugged nonchalantly. The ride was mostly spent quietly listening to music. Every now and then Greg would light a cigarette, and puff hard on it until it was gone, then flick it out his window which was just barely cracked open. Dayna made a couple attempts at striking up a conversation, but Greg did not seem like much of a talker, so she quickly gave up and sat quietly and stared out the window or at her phone for the entire ride. They pulled into the driveway in front of Dayna's old home, a tattered old trailer that was clearly in desperate need of some major repairs.

"Do you need help carrying your things out of there and packing them into the truck?", he asked her thoughtfully. She graciously accepted the help. When they walked in Danny was reclining in his chair in front of the television which was playing a NASCAR race. She knew he was sleeping heavily when she heard his deep rumbling snore. As she expected, her mom was nowhere to be seen either. Dayna figured she was probably already at work, given she did not get very many days off. Dayna put her finger over her lips and pointed over at the sleeping Danny, signaling for Greg to be quiet as they walked past him, being careful to make as little noise as possible. They carefully carried the boxes and furniture out to the truck, making a surprisingly small amount of noise despite the trailer's old creaky floors and the clutter that lay everywhere. After three trips in and out of the trailer, they had completely emptied Dayna's old room and packed everything neatly into the bed of Greg's red truck. Dayna was relieved that they had been able to get it all done without rousing Danny, who likely would have only gotten in the way and made the process take much longer by trying to make conversation with Greg. Greg secured her things with a few tow straps he had conveniently laying around in the truck and they made the return trip, again without much conversation taking place between the two.

When they pulled back into the gravelly driveway of her new place, Greg helped Dayna unload her stuff into the house, setting everything down on the floor of the living room. Then Greg asked her to let him know when she would be ready for company. Dayna thanked him and told him she was just going to get everything set up and take a shower and get ready and then she would text him to tell him he can come back over. He eyed her petite body and long legs once again before turning to leave to get some work done. Dayna heard his truck start with a loud growl and then rumble loudly out of her driveway. She felt overwhelmed as she looked at the pile of stuff on her living room floor. She deflated the air mattress, putting it away on the top shelf of the closet in the bathroom to use if she ever had company staying over and then she replaced it with her bed. She dragged her small white dresser into her room and sat her little twenty-eight-inch flatscreen television she had got for Christmas a couple years ago on top of it, then she unpacked each box finding a place for everything in her new home. She hung any pictures she had on the wall with a few nails she kept in a jar and straightened her rug neatly out on her bedroom floor securing it in place by using the weight of her furniture. She still needed so much furniture, especially for the living room, which was still bare, but the place felt much less empty now that she had all her stuff unpacked and set up. She looked around her place one last time feeling proud. Once she was showered and fresh, Dayna texted Greg to let him know she was ready for him to come back. He showed up about ten minutes later and she let him inside and closed and locked the door behind him.

"Ready?" Greg said, being all business as usual, and he wasted no time with small talk and walked straight back to the room. Dayna completely undressed herself except for her sexy black thong and then leaned back on her bed feeling both nervous and excited. He sat on the end of the bed and removed his work boots carefully as he eyed her naked body with what was clearly a look of satisfaction on his face. First, he pinched her nipple and pulled it lightly. He then trailed his fingertips up her legs, and to that hot spot between her thighs.

"mmm", she moaned, her pussy was already wet and throbbing with anticipation. He pulled her panties down around her ankles leaving her completely exposed and planted a wet kiss right on her pussy. She moaned and thrusted her hips forward as he gently flicked her clit with his tongue. He parted her lips and shoved his tongue inside the tight little hole not far beneath her clit which he was now slowly working open gently with his fingers. She felt another finger press firmly against her asshole using the wetness from his mouth and her pussy as lubricant so he could slip the finger inside. Once he did, his tongue began prodding her asshole as he guided her hand to the bulge that was threatening to burst through the zipper of his pants at any moment.

She undid his jeans obediently and a large fat cock eagerly popped out. He grabbed her hips and guided her on top of him as he flipped her over, placing her pussy on his face with her face in the direction of his cock. She took the whole thing into her mouth and it gagged her as it pushed its way into the back of her throat. He groaned in satisfaction and buried his face deep in her pussy. She began to move her hips, pushing her clit against his tongue as she sucked hard on his cock, repeatedly pushing it into the back of her throat occasionally gagging. Every now and then she momentarily had to come up to catch her breath. He grabbed her ass and used it to guide her tight little asshole to his mouth and she moaned in pleasure as he continued to work her clit with his thumb.

She had no idea having her ass eaten could feel this good when she had tried it before. She had never been this dirty before with someone she barely knew.

This was also the first time she had been fingered in the ass so deeply, so she was going to enjoy the hell out of every second of it. He pulled his finger back slowly and then dove back in hard and fast, fucking her ass like a madman, faster and faster until he pulled his cock from her mouth and shot his cum all over her face and lips. As he continued to come, she put her lips around the head of his cock and sucked some of his cum into her mouth as it dripped from his cock. She quickly licked it off her lips before pulling her mouth back to his cock and sucking it back in.

"Mmmm", she moaned once again as he reached up to her ass with his tongue and began to fuck her mouth like he was fucking her pussy. It was ecstasy. He grabbed her hands and pulled her down flat on top of him and switched to fuck her pussy with his tongue while he pulled on her tits. She squeezed his cock and rubbed her pussy against his face as hard as she could until it suddenly began to tingle and heat up, and she moaned again in ecstasy as she felt herself getting wetter and wetter and had to slow down as she could feel herself coming all over his face. She pulled her pussy away from his mouth and finished her orgasm, as she was overwhelmed with pleasure. She lay on top of him panting, his cock slowly sliding from her mouth.
She felt him rubbing her ass, rubbing her pussy and clit until she finally felt it break through again and that same warm sensation kept coming as it spread over her entire body. She felt her tight pussy spasm again as she licked his balls and moaned in appreciation. He slowly worked her clit in circles with his tongue.

She once again began feeling the same tingle that meant she was close to yet another climax. She moaned and pushed herself hard against his face once more as she came. He tasted as much of the sweet juices as he could, feeling her legs trembling with pleasure. She pulled away unable to take the feeling of growing intensity. He used her hips to lift her off his face and stood up beside the bed and grabbed her hair. He pushed his cock forcefully into her mouth and thrust it in and out until he started to come one more time. He pulled his cock from her mouth and watched as she held her tongue out, lapping up as much of the cum as she could reach with her tongue. He breathed a sigh of satisfaction and looked at her with a pleased expression. When he turned to pull his pants on, she wiped all the remaining cum off her face with a hand towel she had sat on the table near the bed and smiled at him. He was amazed by the fantastic time she gave him, thanked her politely and left. Leaving her feeling satisfied and tired, she put on the television and fell fast asleep within minutes.

Dayna looked at Ella in anticipation wondering if Ella would think badly of her because she used sexual favors to barter a way to get her stuff. Dayna had not had anyone to confide in in the last six years when she broke down and told her close friend Jessica all about her wild lifestyle. In the end that did not turn out well at all, and she nearly lost custody of her son. As a result, Dayna remains tight-lipped about certain parts of her life to everyone, and that often made her feel isolated. She studied Ella's expression actively trying to spot any signs of disapproval. Ella did not seem at all phased by the story.

"Wow! So, he did you have any more bedroom encounters with him?", Ella asked.

"Just the one", Dayna responded, "he never made another move, and I think he did stuff like that a lot, because after that I was always seeing him with different women".

"So, after that y'all's relationship remained strictly business, about the apartment I mean", Ella said as she stacked their empty plates neatly on the table. Dayna nodded. "I had a sugar daddy in college for a while", Ella laughed at the memory fondly. She told Dayna how easy he made things for her financially, and about the social perks it had as well. He gave her a lot of his connections too, which have proven to be infinitely valuable. She had been strapped for cash at the time because a year or so prior Ella's dad got sick.

"I'm sorry to hear that", Dayna said sadly. Ella told her that soon after her mom had stopped paying for college because her dad's medical expenses were piling up, so she got a job. Juggling work and school proved to be more than she could handle, so when her friend told her about her own success with a sugar daddy website, she signed up immediately. It did not take long for her to meet someone too. By this point Dayna had relaxed and decided that she could trust Ella completely. She did not feel like Ella was the type to judge others too harshly.

"I'm not going to lie, I really got into the whole being a sugar baby thing right away. He was older but not so older that it was gross or anything", she explained. "In fact, he was really in shape and fun, and there's something about being with an older man that I really enjoyed", she said as she dove straight into her next story.

Ella Gets Punished (spanking)

"Yeah?", Ella groggily murmured, lifting her head from the table. She had her arms shielded around her to block out the light that shone through the window. When she saw where she was, she quickly sat upright and looked around to see if anyone, besides the person who woke her up, had been paying attention. Luckily, the library was mostly empty.

"Are you okay?", Fallon asked looking concerned.

"Yeah, I worked late last night, so I hardly got any sleep", Ella explained groggily as she wiped the crust from her eyes.

Fallon nodded at her with a look of concern still on her face and suggested Ella take a break from studying and go with her to meet a couple friends at the cafe for something caffeinated. Ella agreed and started slowly stacking the books on the corner of the table and packed her notebook and pens into her bag. The whole way to the cafe Ella complained to Fallon about the waitressing job she took on to pay for her tuition. Fallon looked at her sympathetically for a moment before her eyes widened.

"I have an idea", Fallon said excitedly. "Maybe you should talk to Hannah, she told me something about getting help from some website to pay for tuition, and she said she doesn't have to pay it back either", she suggested. Ella knew she needed something like that badly, so she decided she would approach Hannah about it as soon as she got a chance. She did not know how she could possibly make it like this till the end of the semester, let alone to the completion of her degree. Working long hours at a physically demanding job, and then going to school to pursue a degree program that is also demanding was really an impossibly heavy load. Luckily, her chance to speak with Hannah came almost immediately, Ella saw her sitting at the cafe in the group's regular spot, her laptop was opened in front of her as she typed ferociously on the keyboard. Ella sat in the seat right across from her and Fallon took the seat beside her.

Before Ella could even think of what to say, Fallon blurted, "Hey Hannah, I was just telling Ella how you were getting help with your tuition on that website you mentioned earlier. She could probably use something like that herself". Ella's cheeks turned slightly red with embarrassment. Hannah looked up from her computer and smiled a tight sympathetic smile at Ella. She asked Ella if she had time to talk about it a little later. She said she was working on something that was due later today, so she did not have time to tell her about it at this moment. Ella told her that would be fine and asked her to let her know whenever she had a chance. Fallon started telling everyone bye as soon as she got her coffee, she had a class starting soon, so she left Ella at the cafe to hurry off to get to her class. Ella sat and sipped on the latte she ordered as she read over the notes, she had taken in the library in preparation for a test she had the next day. Even though she had finished most of the latte already, Ella was struggling to keep her eyes open. Hannah noticed Ella opening and closing her eyes.

"Here", Hannah said, handing her a bottle of pills. Ella looked at the bottle suspiciously, when she saw they said caffeine on the bottle she opened it and took one. She thanked Hannah and tried to give them back, but Hannah refused. She asked Ella if she wanted to walk with her back to the main building, and Ella agreed. Both girls began shoving things into their bags. Ella had made up her mind to head back to the dorm and get a power nap in before her psychology class anyway. She knew if she did not, she would most likely fall asleep during class and she preferred to not embarrass herself anymore by falling asleep in random places. Both girls finished gathering their stuff and stood to leave. Ella thanked Hannah for taking the time to help her. Hannah said she did not mind at all and they started towards the main building.

"I'd really appreciate it if you don't tell anyone that I told you about this", Hannah said quietly. Ella was confused and curious so she promised Hannah that she would not tell anyone. Hannah explained that she had been getting help with her tuition from a sugar daddy she met online. She told Ella that there were tons of local men on this site looking for young, beautiful girls to spoil. As Ella listened her jaw nearly dropped. This was not at all the kind of help Ella had been expecting, but she needed it badly, so she took the scrap of paper Hannah gave her with the website on it. When Ella made it back to the dorm, she set her alarm and crawled straight into bed falling immediately asleep.

The alarm clock abruptly jarred Ella awake, she sat up in bed and immediately started getting herself ready for class. After brushing her hair and touching up her makeup, she thought about the website Hannah had given her and realized she was a bit excited about the prospect of having a sugar daddy. She made her way to psychology class in a hurry, barely making it on time, and when class was over, she was eager to get started with making her profile. She meticulously filled everything out. She took her time deciding on the right username and bio for her profile. She used a photo she took for Brennon last semester as her profile picture. It was one of her favorite pictures of herself. In it she had on a black Lace crop top that exposed her flat stomach, and tight jeans that made her ass look perfectly round. Then she selected a few other sexy pics to use on her profile. Once she finished setting it up, she turned over and closed her eyes to finish catching up on some much-needed rest.

When she awoke, she was surprised to see that she already had four messages from potential sugar daddies. She checked them one by one, she read the messages in the order she had received them. Two of them were from the same sender, he seemed a little creepy and desperate. His first message asking if she wanted to fuck, and the second was an unwelcome dick pic. She frowned at her computer screen and quickly blocked the sender. Then there was one from a man who looked old enough to be her grandfather. She shuddered a little, and decided she just could not do that, so she blocked that sender as well. She moved on to the next message already feeling a little discouraged. This guy was older too, but still extremely attractive. He wore an expensive suite in his profile photo, he looked like he was in good shape, and he also had a wonderful smile. His message was written in a very formal tone. In it he invited her to have dinner with him at a nice restaurant. His message said his name was Shaun. She typed a message back accepting Shaun's invitation, and they set up a time to meet. It was just three days away, which gave her mixed feelings of anxiousness and exhilaration.

Over the next three days she continued checking her messages on the site for potential sugar daddies, but none seemed as interesting as her Friday night date seemed. She responded to a few guys, just in case this one did not work out for whatever reason, but she avoided making any other plans just yet. She did not tell Fallon or anyone else what she was planning to do. She kept it to herself as Hannah had asked her to do, also because she was a little worried about what the others might think of her. She did have another conversation with Hannah about it though. Hannah told her that each man would have different expectations, but most would expect some form of sexual favor. She said that she often got expensive gifts and was taken out on fancy dates and even an occasional trip, that all came on top of having her tuition completely covered. Later, Ella logged onto the site to check her messages again. Shaun had sent her a message to confirm their date the following day, he included his cell phone number and asked her to text him her response when she could. Ella saved Shaun's number in her phone and sent a text that said, "I can't wait to meet you tomorrow. Ella". She had trouble sleeping that night because she was so excited about the upcoming date. Ella got out of bed still feeling exhausted from working and attending school. She could hardly pay attention in any of her classes due to the exhaustion and excitement. She bolted out of her last class, speed-walking to her dorm as quickly as possible to ensure she had ample time to get herself ready for the upcoming date. Upon making it to her dorm, she picked up a dress she had laid across her bed that morning. It was red and trimmed with lace, the heart shaped top was classy and sexy, it was tight around her waist and the skirt flowed off her waist stopping at her thighs. She happily noticed how smooth and tanned her legs were. She put on some music and got to work on her hair. She moved her hips to the music as she applied her makeup. Before leaving the bathroom, she spritzed herself with her favorite perfume. Shortly after she finished getting ready her phone dinged. It was her date letting her know he was about to come pick her up. She had told him that she could meet him at the restaurant, but he insisted on picking her up. She figured his age was the cause of his insistence on picking her up. She was already waiting outside when she saw the deep red Lexus LC pull up in front of her dorm building. She looked around to see what attention the genuinely nice, and expensive car had attracted. All over the parking lot and in front of the building people looked up to notice the striking car, and to see who was getting into it.

Excitement bubbled up as she walked towards the door. A handsome older gentleman quickly got out of the car and ran around the car to open her door. He took her hand and gestured her into the car. She slid into the leather seat and marveled at its perfectly shiny interior. Shaun got back into the driver seat and looked at her and smiled with the whitest teeth she had ever seen.

"Your photos don't do you justice"' he said to her politely. He held out his hand and when she went to take it, he lifted her hand to his lips and softly kissed it. She returned his smile and thanked him. She buckled her seatbelt securely around her hips as he returned his attention to the road. They made small talk on the short drive to the restaurant. She talked about her classes and friends. He told her about his job as the COO of a major home security company. They pulled up to a contemporary looking restaurant called Aria. She had heard a few people talk about it at school, but she had never been. It was much too expensive for her. Shaun exited the car and made his way to open the door for her again. She took the hand he offered and got out of the car and walked inside with her arm looped into his. She noticed how great it felt to be treated this way. He seemed like such a gentleman, and it made him very charming.

The hostess took their jackets before seating them at a private table in the corner of the restaurant. She asked them each if they prefer sparkling water or still water. Shaun asked for still. Ella was not sure what that meant at first, so she asked for still as well. When the waitress got to their table, he ordered a bottle of wine. They sat sipping wine and looking over the menu. He ordered a prime rib, and she had the Chilean Sea Bass. They were having a great time eating, drinking, talking, and laughing. The food was delicious, and Shaun was funny, and down-to-earth. She started feeling the effects of the wine shortly after the second bottle was opened. Her glances at him became more and more flirty as she started to feel a warmth in her stomach and her pussy. That warmth turned to heat when she felt Shaun's hand lightly touching her thigh under the table. She opened her legs slightly and he eyed her with hungry eyes. He ran his hand up the inside of her thigh until it reached her panties. He rubbed the top of her panties, feeling the warmth and wetness. As he explored her pussy with his fingers, he asked if she wanted dessert, as if nothing were happening under the table, and she politely declined saying she was far too full.

Shaun requested the check, and when the waitress returned, he handed her his card without looking at the bill. Before standing to leave he threw a bunch of twenties down on the table. Ella was impressed by the tip he had left. When they returned to his car, he asked Ella if she would like to take a detour to go by his place to have one more drink before he returned her to her dorm. She smiled at him knowingly before happily accepting his offer and after a twenty-minute ride of more polite conversation, they pulled into a genuinely nice upscale neighborhood of huge houses and then up to a large 2-story house on a very private lot towards the back of the neighborhood.

Shaun helped her out of the car and walked her to the front door and then inside. The inside of the house was as beautiful as it was on the outside, and it was exceptionally large, and very well decorated. He immediately walked over to a wooden liquor cabinet and asked her if she drank brandy. She never had, but she said yes so, he poured her some over a glass of ice. She took a big drink and then sipped it carefully after realizing how strong it was. Shaun watched her looking amused.

"You're a very bad girl", he remarked plainly.

"Excuse me?", Ella responded, not sure if she had heard him correctly.

"You let a stranger touch your pretty little pussy in the middle of an upscale restaurant.
That makes you an unbelievably bad girl", he repeated to her. She did not know what to say. Her words were caught in her throat. Her pussy got wetter, even though she became suddenly nervous.

"I..uh…" She stuttered unsure of what to say.

"I'm going to punish you", He stated, cutting her off without much emotion. He walked over to her and grabbed her firmly by the wrist. She did not object or pull away as he led her into a bedroom with a perfectly made bed. He walked her over to the side of a made-up bed with a deep red comforter. "Bend over", he said looking at her authoritatively.

"But- "she started to object.
"Do as you're told", he interjected in a demanding tone. She looked at him and obediently bent over the side of the bed as she felt a dizzying feeling of excitement, fear, and

pleasure. She felt a stinging feeling and heard a loud pop as his hand met her ass. "A sexy little bad girl", he remarked as he rubbed her beautiful plump ass with the hand he had just smacked her with. She moaned a little in anticipation of more. He ordered her to pull the skirt of her dress around her waist, and she did as she was told. He smacked her again, hard, she whimpered a little as he pulled her panties off her hips and let them fall around her ankles. He smacked her ass once again. Her face was now flushed and hot and she felt that her pussy was so wet it might start dripping at any moment. She felt his hand slide between her legs. He used his hand to pry her legs further apart before smacking her again, hard on her supple ass. His hand reached up and pinched her nipple through her dress and he softly chuckled.

"I guess I like my girls a little bad", he said. He smacked her bare ass again. It was on fire at this point. His hand felt warm as he rubbed away the sting. "Are you my girl? he asked, putting emphasis on 'my'.

"Yes", she muttered breathlessly. He smacked her again. The pain was terrific. It was beginning to feel like fire every time his hand hit her smooth flesh.

"Yes what?", he asked.

"Yes sir", she said more loudly this time. She felt exposed as he paused a moment. She heard him rummaging around for something before it went quiet again. He struck her again but this time it was not his hand that hit her ass. It was hard and flat and rough. He struck her again and again. Each blow made her pussy wetter and her ass sting more. She wanted to scream but it was caught in her throat. She wondered if her ass was blistered. She felt it must be. She was not sure how many blows she had endured. It stopped again and he plunged his fingers deep into her pussy. She came almost right away. Squirming against the bed as he pounded his fingers deep inside her. When her orgasm stopped, so did he. He walked across the room and she saw him wipe his hands on a hand towel from the corner of her eye. Moments later, he came back and pulled his pants and underwear down to the floor and pulled a red blindfold out of a drawer and held it in front of her face.

"Your naughtiness, little girl, is cause for some punishment", he said, pulling the blindfold over her eyes. She felt the cold wood of what she now recognized as a paddle as he slowly smacked her bare ass over and over. The sting was unreal, the sting was everywhere, and it was painful, yet for a reason unbeknown to her, she enjoyed each second of it. He slapped her ass as hard as he could, and she flinched from the intense, powerful stings and the windiness that hit her pussy and spread up into her chest. He slapped her ass for a long time, and then he ordered her to kneel on the floor, where he began to slap her tits with a flogger he had tucked under his bed. He felt her spasm from the biting pain and her pussy get wetter. She moaned and whimpered at the terrible, painful stings on her body, and he knew she was enjoying it, even though she did not admit it to him, yet.

"Harder daddy", she begged. He grabbed her pussy and stuck two fingers deep inside her pussy. The feeling was incredible as he flicked his finger over her clit, catching it with his hand. The initial pain of the paddle on her ass and her pussy had made her so wet that she needed a lot more pressure on her clit before she could cum. The delicious pleasure of his finger rubbing over her clit was almost more than she could stand, yet he would not let her cum yet, as he knew she would be spanked again at a later time. "You are my good girl. Your safe place is with me, and I am going to keep it that way", he said.

"Faster daddy, faster", she begged as he slapped her ass again. The paddle landed hard against the wooden floor and the sound of it made her wetter. The pain was intense but now that it was coming, it made her forget everything else. She felt such a sweet release as he slapped her again with his bare hand and she came again as he rubbed his fingers deep inside her pussy, then he tenderly rubbed her ass, she could not take any more thankfully he was satisfied as well. She lay naked on the bed crying, her ass, much like her eyes, was red and puffy from the paddling.

"You can get up now sweetheart", he urged with a cool tone. Ella stood wiping her eyes and bent to grab her panties. She balled them into her fist and pulled her dress back down over her stinging ass. "The restroom is over there if you'd like to freshen up", he said as he gestured to a door on the other side of the room. She sheepishly walked over to it. She immediately examined her bottom in the mirror above the double vanity. She gasped at the sight, her skin was a deep red, almost purple color, and there were welts all across her swollen cheeks. It stung and was hot to the touch. She noticed a clean hand towel folded neatly on the corner of the vanity. She picked it up and wet it with soapy water and wiped her own cum off her pussy with it. She grabbed another towel she found in the drawer and used it to wipe up the eyeliner and tears that ran down her puffy face. When she was done her heart began to pound as she went to leave the restroom. She was not sure what she would say or how she would act when she saw him. When she opened the door, the room was empty.

"I'm in here", Shaun's voice called from the main room. She followed his voice into the foyer where they had come in. He already had his jacket on and was holding hers out politely offering to help her put it on. Without saying anything. she turned around and slipped her arms into the sleeves. He opened the door and she quietly followed him out to the car. She was completely exhausted when she made it back to her dorm. She had plans to go out with a few of her friends, but she called and canceled explaining that she was just too tired to go out. She slept great that night. She dreamed about her encounter with Shaun except in her dream he fucked her with his hard cock. When she awoke, she was still in a daze and trying to process yesterday's events. Her ass still had a slight redness to it. She was not sure why, but she had really enjoyed getting spanked by Shaun. She could not wait to see him again. Ella checked her student email as she did every morning. There was a message from the school's financial department. It notified her that her semester's tuition had been paid in full. She held her hand over her mouth to try to contain the excited squeal that she let slip out.

"I cannot wait to quit that miserable job I have", she thought with satisfaction. She felt relieved and renewed knowing she no longer had to worry about how she was going to cover her tuition. She was surprised by the fact that she did not feel the least bit guilty for accepting payment in exchange for sexual favors. She genuinely liked Shaun and the spanking he gave her had made a switch flip inside of her as she realized that she loved being dominated. She was excited to move forward with this endeavor and wondered what other treats this arrangement might include, or if he would take her on vacations to places she had never been. She had seen these types of arrangements on television, and it felt incredibly exciting to now be a part of one herself now.

Dayna felt so relieved that Ella had an experience that opened her mind to that sort of thing. At this point they were both catching a buzz and being a lot more forthcoming about their lives to one another. They were having a great time sharing their stories and learning more about the other's experiences.

"So that was your first time with an older man?", Dayna asked.

Ella nodded and said that it was. Ella was surprised by how much she was comfortable sharing with Dayna. Normally Ella was diligent about keeping up her appearances. For her mom, for her coworkers, and all her so-called friends who really knew nothing about who she was. Ella realized that since Dayna and she had graduated, she had not had a single real friend, no one to confide in. Ella looked across the table at Dayna and smiled. "I hope this friendship lasts", Ella thought. As she reminisced with Dayna about their innocent, and conservative ways as teenagers. She found it so funny how they both blossomed into adults with some wild and crazy sexual experiences. Dayna asked the bartender to get them another round. She checked her phone to make sure she had no messages from the babysitter.

"What do you have there?", Ella asked, glancing over, "texting a boyfriend?".

"No, I'm currently single", Dayna said, shaking her head. She told Ella she was making sure her son was okay with the sitter. She had paid the babysitter for the full night just in case but told her she might be home early depending on how things go. In light of how well things were going, Dayna decided to send her a text to let her know not to expect her home till late tonight or early morning. Once she got a response, she returned her phone to her purse, and her attention to Ella. Ella asked so she told her all about Brady, her son.

"I don't have any kids, and I don't really plan to", Ella said as if she were imagining what it would be like, "my job is way too demanding".

Dayna explained that she had not really planned it either, "It just happened", she shrugged.

"Is the dad around?", Ella asked.

Dayna shook her head, "I let him know I was pregnant, but I never heard from him after that". Ella continued prodding for information about Brady's father. Dayna did not mind because they were never really in a relationship. In fact, they were only in contact for a very brief time. So, Dayna decided to use her turn as storyteller to tell Ella the story about how she had ended up pregnant at such a young age and without the father's help.

Dayna Is Sweet as Pie

(cream pie)

It was a beautiful day outside; Dayna had just finished cleaning up her house. She recently rented out a room to her friend, Tori. Dayna could hear Tori in the other room just waking up. She was in her room loudly getting ready as she did every morning, sometimes at oddly early hours due to her job. She turned the music up to drown Tori's noise out and sat on the couch as she carefully sipped her coffee and packed the bong full of weed. She mindlessly flipped through a book she had been intending to read for a while now. She propped her feet up on the coffee table, put the bong to her mouth, and began to light the weed on fire. Suddenly, as if she could already smell it burning, Tori burst through her bedroom door and into the hallway.

"Hey bitch", Tori greeted her in the usual way.

"What's up slut", Dayna replied.

"Have you packed the bowl yet?", Tori asked but before Dayna could even respond she started again, "Oh and I have a few new friends coming by in a bit. They said they had some good shit".

Dayna held her hand out with the loaded bong and told Tori to come smoke with her. They sat on the couch together and smoked. Tori asked Dayna if she wanted to come to a party and bonfire by the creek with her tomorrow. They had these things often and Dayna seldom went. As usual, Dayna politely declined because she really did not enjoy those things. People get drunk and fight and everyone is always acting ridiculous. Dayna worried about stuff like that getting her into trouble she did not need to be in. Both girls got startled when they heard a knock on the door. They looked at each other and laughed as Tori yelled for her visitors to come inside. The door opened and three people noisily entered their house. The first was a guy with a couple missing teeth that looked to be in his thirties wearing a Marlboro shirt, a woman who also appeared to be in her thirties and appeared to be strung out on drugs. She had brown frizzy hair and was very thin. Her arm was looped into the arm of the guy with the Marlboro shirt, as she possessively eyed Dayna and Tori. Behind them, a very good-looking guy that appeared to be in his early twenties. Tori invited them all to sit down. The couple sat in the recliner together and Tori and Dayna scooted down the couch to make room for the younger guy, who sat down on the end beside Dayna. Tori introduced the couple as Scott, and Renee.

"I haven't met this one", Tori said, eyeing the younger guy.

"That's my brother Jesse", Scott said dismissively as he held out his hand to Renee. She immediately dug into her black purse and revealed a gallon sized Ziplock bag of marijuana.

"Whew!", Tori exclaimed loudly, "I can smell it from here".

Dayna had not even paid much attention to the bud. She was somewhat distracted by the younger guy, Jesse. She had complimented the tribal tattoo on his arm. He thanked her and they immediately began telling one another all about their tattoos. Dayna was brought back to reality when Tori tapped on her arm to get her attention and immediately shoved the newly packed bong in her direction. Dayna hit it and blew out a huge cloud of smoke, then passed it over to Jesse, who hit it once and passed it along. Tori handed Scott a wad of cash, who then pulled out some scales and weighed some of the weed out onto the tray and poured it into a small bag. He passed it to Tori, and immediately said he had somewhere to be, so he stood up to leave.

"C'mon Jesse", Scott said. Dayna reluctantly said bye to Jesse and all three left without saying much more. As soon as they walked out the door Dayna turned to Tori with excited wide eyes.

"Omg! I call dibs on that hottie Jesse", she said quickly.

"Does this mean you're going to the bonfire tomorrow?", Tori asked teasingly.

Dayna asked if he would be there and Tori told Dayna that she had invited Scott and Renee, and they said they would come, so there was a good chance he would be there as well. Dayna sighed and reluctantly agreed to go, "but if he's not there, I'm probably going to come back here", she said, "you know I hate going to those things". Tori rolled her eyes at Dayna as she grabbed the remote and put on a movie for them. They sat quietly on the couch watching television together with their legs tangled together as they smoked some of the green Tori just bought. The day was quiet and lazy because it was one of the rare occasions neither of them had to work. Dayna could not help but feel giddy over Jesse. She really hoped he would be at the bonfire tomorrow. She sat and planned her approach in her mind as the movie played in the background. She thought about what she would say to him and imagined how he would respond. Jesse was the first person in a while that she felt this attracted to. Dayna and Tori hung out the rest of the day just watching movies, relaxing, and getting high.

The next morning Dayna hopped out of bed with more energy than normal and made herself some coffee. She called her mom and talked to her for over an hour as she slowly sipped on her coffee. Tori had left for work super early that morning so Dayna hoped she would get home early too. She walked into the house around two in the afternoon, and immediately sat on the couch by Dayna as she usually did. Dayna packed the bowl completely full and passed it over to Tori. Tori was more excited than she usually was about these parties, because this time, Dayna would be coming along with her, and lately that was exceptionally rare. The two girls got ready together, helping one another with makeup and critiquing each other's outfits. Dayna and Tori both decided on bikini tops and jean shorts. It was summer and they both wanted to turn heads. When they were both ready, they sat down and smoked some more till it was time to leave. Dayna decided to have a few pre-game drinks to build up her courage as well. They got in Tori's truck and left. Both were feeling excited about the upcoming evening. When they pulled up to the party, they saw a bunch of coolers littering the bank of the creek, in which each group had their preference of beer and maybe a few bottles of liquor too. Tori also brought a cooler for herself and Dayna, which remained in the bed of her truck.

Tori looked at Dayna and smiled, "Ready?", she asked.

"I guess", Dayna replied with an exasperated sigh.
Both girls got out of the truck and Tori grabbed them each a beer out of the cooler. Dayna popped hers open the second Tori passed it to her. She chugged nearly half of it down right away. Dayna quietly followed Tori around and they mingled with everyone at the party. There was a whole pig cooking in a smoker a group of guys made in the ground. The smell made Dayna's stomach growl. She kept searching for Jesse as they made their way down the creek. She was talking to an acquaintance when Tori grabbed and shook her arm. She pointed in the direction they had walked from and there was a truck parking right beside Tori's. Tori mouthed Scott's name as she pointed at the truck. So, Dayna watched hoping Jesse would get out of it. When she saw him, she thought of the ways he would be touching her by the end of the night. Her pussy got a little wet and her nipples perked up beneath her bikini top. She made her way back towards Tori's truck to meet Jesse. He looked her up and down and flirtatiously smiled when he saw Dayna walk up. She returned his smile as she approached him.

"Hey", she said with her hand held over her eyes to shield them from the bright sun, "what's up?". He examined the tattoo on her ribs,

"I can actually see it now, I really like it", he said of the floral tattoo on her rib cage as he trailed his fingers along the morning glories and vines that went down to her hip. His touch made her body react immediately. She looked at him wondering if he had noticed, he looked back at her with that same seductive smile. He offered her a shot from a flask he had in his pocket. She took a swig without asking what it was. Her face scrunched up when the taste of whiskey hit her. He laughed at the face she made.

"Sorry, I guess I should've warned you", he said, "that's some strong shit".

"That's okay", she said through a cough. They walked around together talking and drinking. There were a couple times when she thought he might have been flirting with her, but she was unsure. She wondered if he noticed her attempts at flirting with him. They mostly hung out amongst themselves until the sun started going down. They saw that a crowd was beginning to form around where the pig had been cooking, and they figured it might be ready. They made their way towards the crowd to get a plate of food.

As everyone finished eating, the party's energy seemed to be hyping up tremendously. The sun began to disappear behind the tops of the trees and all the parents began dutifully loading their children up to head home for the night. A single huge speaker appeared near the bonfire and began filling the air with intoxicating beats. A crowd of dancing people began to form around the speaker. They moved to the rhythm of the music with their bodies pressed against one another. Everyone appeared to be having a great time. Even Dayna was feeling the vibe as Jesse began to lead her toward the crowd. They got close enough to the speaker that they could feel the vibrations. Jesse pulled Dayna close, she felt the alcohol making her head buzz and her body warm. She moved her body against his seductively. She felt his hard cock as she rubbed her ass against it. His hands began exploring her body. They danced and laughed among the crowd of people for what felt like eternity. When they stopped, they were sweaty and completely out of breath. They decided to walk back to the trucks to get a drink.

Jessie retrieved two beers from the cooler and handed one of them to Dayna. He pulled the tailgate down on his brother's truck and they both sat on it. Jesse felt more confident thanks to the buzz he now had, so he reached his hand around Dayna's waist to pull her closer to him. She looked up at him with a huge grin and he leaned in to kiss Dayna's lips. The second their lips met they both dove into their desires. The chemistry between them that had been building up was enhanced by the alcoholic stupor they both found themselves in. He parted her lips with his thumb and pushed his tongue inside her mouth. Dayna responded with a moan as she arched her back to get her body closer to his. He began to use his hands to feel all over her body. She grabbed his hand to put it under the shirt that the night's chill made her put on not long ago. This was her way of letting him know that he could explore beneath her clothes as well. Dayna could feel that her pussy was very wet now, and it tingled in anticipation. She put her hand where Jesse's cock was. She felt that it was hard for her and it pressed tight against his pants, threatening to bust free. As Dayna rubbed his cock through Jesse's jeans he grabbed and played with her tits.

Seemingly at the same time they both stopped and looked around suddenly remembering where they were. They smiled at each other looking both guilty and disappointed. "We can leave if you want", Dayna suggested looking at Jesse seductively, "I can take Tori's truck and come back and pick her up or your brother can drop her at my place and pick you up". Jesse texted his brother to let him know where he was going and asked him if he could bring Tori home and pick him up there. As he did that Dayna ran to find Tori and get the keys to her truck. Scott agreed to bring Tori home and Dayna successfully got the keys from a very drunk Tori who was grinding on some random guys. She got in and began grabbing stuff from the passenger seat and setting it on the floor. Jesse opened the passenger door just as she had finished clearing the seat and she started the truck. The engine roared to life causing the entire truck to shake and vibrate. It felt good against her wet and already tingly pussy.

They talked and flirted relentlessly with each other as Dayna drove them back to the house. Every now and then she would cuss at the truck for making a questionable noise or jerking unexpectedly. She hated driving Tori's truck, because she was always afraid it would quit on her, but she supposed it was worth it this time. Jesse eyed her the whole way, and Dayna glanced over at him as much as she could. When their eyes met, they would grin at one another as if they were sharing an inside joke. They were both anticipating the sex that would surely take place once they got to Dayna and Tori's place. Dayna pulled into the driveway and parked the car as close to the house as she could. She unlocked the front door and threw her keys on the table as she let Jesse in the door. Before making their way into Dayna's room, both Dayna and Jesse needed to use the restroom. Dayna fixed them both a drink while she waited for Jesse to come out, and once he did, she ushered him into her room and closed the door. Jesse immediately resumed kissing Dayna. She moaned and pressed her body against him. She pushed him backwards onto her bed as their lips remained locked and their tongues swirled around each other.

Jesse grabbed the bottom of her t-shirt and pulled it over her head. She did the same pulling his shirt off and exposing his bare chest which was beautifully defined. She noticed that he was perfectly sculpted and tanned. He cupped her boobs in his hand through the bikini top she was still wearing. Jesse reached behind Dayna and pulled the string on her bikini top. It untied easily and it fell straight to the floor, exposing Dayna's chest. He cupped both of her boobs in his hands again but this time he leaned in and pulled one of her nipples into his mouth. Dayna eagerly began to undo the button of Jesse's pants. She had only gotten the button unclasped before he began kissing his way down her flat stomach, which made it impossible to remove his pants. He grabbed the top of her pants instead, after getting the button undone, he pulled her pants off, and threw them to the bedroom floor with her panties still on, he kissed her where her sex was, she arched her back readily.

Jesse slowly ran his tongue across her clit in a circular motion. Dayna let a sigh of pleasure escape from her lips. Her pussy was slick with a mixture of her juices, and his spit. It felt hot and ready for Jesse's cock. He stood and removed his jeans gazing intently at a naked Dayna lying on the bed. Her pussy wanted his cock so bad, but she wanted to feel it in her mouth too. She sat up on the bed and took his rigid cock first in her hand and then she brought it to her mouth. She heaved a little when he thrusted his hips forward, forcing it completely into her mouth. He groaned and ran his fingers through her hair. For a moment, he watched Dayna's head undulate as she sucked and licked him vicariously. When he was ready to bury himself in her pussy, he told her to lie back. She obeyed him without a word and looked up at him. He positioned himself between her legs and rubbed his cock against her pussy. He groaned when he felt that it was wet and ready for him. He could not help but to thrust himself deep inside of her tight little pussy. Dayna felt a dizzying pleasure as he repeatedly slammed his dick into her. She wrapped her legs tight around his and cried out in pleasure. Her pussy squeezed his cock as he pushed himself deeper. It felt better than anything he had ever experienced.

They were both completely captivated by one another and the pleasure they were giving and receiving. Dayna's moans, and squeals got more and more intense as she got closer to her climax. She began squirming beneath him and trembling as a feeling of ecstasy swept over her body. His thrusts were getting faster, harder, and deeper. Her mind exploded with pleasure and just seconds later so did his. She felt his cum rush into her, filling her pussy. He relaxed and began panting in exhaustion. He began to realize what he had done as he pulled his cock out and saw some of his cum dripping from her pussy. Dayna sat up and looked down at the cum leaking out in between her legs.

"Shit! I'm not on birth control", she said looking nervous. Jesse felt guilty, knowing what a slut he was being. He knew that he had come in her, and that he had fucked her in her pussy while she was not on any form of birth control. He thought to himself that he would rather have done that with some little slut than with the married woman.

"I can't believe I just did that!" Dayna exclaimed.

"I can't believe it, either," Jesse replied laughing nervously.

Jesse stood up and ran his hand over his cock and it was still rock hard. He walked up to Dayna and kissed her passionately. She opened her mouth, allowing him to take the kiss deeper. They both knelt and kissed each other and touched their tongues together. They laid down in the bed holding each other for a while. Jesse noticed Dayna's breasts rising and falling rapidly. She placed her hands on his chest and then pulled him down to her mouth. She kissed him deeply and lovingly. After a few minutes of passionate kissing, Jesse sat up. He made a deal with himself, he thought, that he would not sleep with Dayna again. He would let her think about it and enjoy it as much as she could, and then move on to her next lover. Jesse got up and went to the bathroom and brushed his teeth. He washed his face and combed his hair. He grabbed a couple of towels and wrapped them around his waist and headed back to the bed. As he got up on the bed, he noticed that Dayna was lying in the bed naked. Jesse lay down beside her and wrapped his arms around her. He kissed the top of her head.

"Jesse?", Dayna whispered in an anxious voice.

"Yeah."

"You are amazing", she whispered lustfully.

"You might be the only person who thinks so, and I doubt you'll think that for very long" Jesse said with a soft chuckle.

Dayna frowned and thought to herself about what Jesse had just said to her. She wondered what would happen if she turned out to be pregnant. She wondered if Jesse would stick around. What was she going to do? "What if I end up pregnant?", she asked.

"I don't know, Dayna. I suppose I would prefer you get it aborted. I am not ready for a kid", Jesse replied in a soft voice.

"Oh", she replied unsure of how she felt about that.

"It is kind of weird, but I know that you are a good girl, and that you will do what is right", Jesse said softly. She pondered the though in her mind. "Don't worry anymore. It will work out", Jesse whispered in her ear. Dayna began to kiss Jesse's neck. She pulled his head back and looked deeply into his eyes. She felt Jesse's cock getting hard against her thigh. She leaned down and began to kiss his chest. Jesse felt Dayna's lips move over the top of his chest and then lower to his belly button. She kissed the bottom of his belly and her tongue gently began to move along the inside of his belly button. She pulled her tongue out and started to lick down his pelvic bone. Jesse felt her tongue sliding across his skin. Jesse could not control himself any longer, and he began to lean over to grab her by her hips.

As Dayna felt Jesse lean over, she felt the warmth of his breath against her pussy. She inhaled deeply and the smell of his cologne was suddenly overwhelming. It was so strong that it made her feel warm all over. Jesse's breath felt like a cool breeze against her pussy and she felt her pussy begin to moisten again. She quickly reached down and grabbed his cock, massaging it in her hand. His cock was fully erect. He noticed how huge it looked in her tiny hands. Dayna grabbed Jesse's cock with her other hand as well and then spread her legs and rubbed her pussy across Jesse's cock. Jesse looked down at her beautiful naked body. He loved the way her long legs felt against him when they wrapped around his waist as he began to fuck her again deeply. He leaned back and lifted her on top of him. He watched, admiring her beauty as she rode him as hard and fast as she could manage. He came in her again as he thrusted his hips forward to get deeper inside of her.

"I'm so sorry", he apologized again looking ashamed. Dayna just shrugged. They talked and after discussing it they both decided that everything should be fine. If she did end up pregnant, they decided that Dayna would just abort it. Dayna tried not to think about it as she packed a bowl. They smoked until Scott showed up to get Jesse, leaving a very drunk Tori in exchange.

"That's how I ended up pregnant with Brady", Dayna said, "I went to the clinic, but I couldn't go through with it. I told Jesse, but he wanted no part of it. I haven't heard from him since".

Ella had seen things like this happen before. That is another reason she did not want to be a mom, so many women end up raising kids alone. Ella liked her freedom and the ability to make decisions without considering anyone else. Dayna clarified that although she may not have planned her son, he was the light of her life and she could not imagine life without him. Both girls jotted to the bathroom to relieve their full bladders after all those drinks. They chirped and chatted and took turns in the single stall and then washed their hands. Dayna showed Ella her stretch marks, which Ella could hardly see. They returned to the table and resumed talking with each other. Dayna asked Ella if she had ever had anal sex.

Ella nodded firmly. "It took me a while to actually try it because I heard it was painful, but once I did, I started to like it. You just get used to it", she explained. For me it enhances sex.

"Yeah, I didn't like it the first time, but once I got used to it, I couldn't get enough", Dayna said in agreement. They both admitted to being terrified the first time trying it, but within a year of their first experience, both had become total butt sluts. They laughed about each other's embarrassing moments and mishaps that happened while they discovered anal sex.

"I really only tried it because I wanted to get back at one of the worst bosses I've ever had", Ella said as she sipped on her drink some more, "It was the first internship I had out of college".

"This sounds like it's going to be a very interesting story", Dayna said as she rested her hands on her arms and looked at Ella to show she was listening intently.

Ella's Backdoor Gets Opened (First Time Anal)

Ella walked into the office for her first day of her internship as a design manager for an engineering company. She was almost an hour early because Shaun had pulled strings to get her this internship, and she did not want to disappoint him. She wore a flowing gray cardigan, over a black tank top with some silky black slacks. Her chunky gray necklace and black pumps perfected the look. She was dressed very business-appropriately yet her outfit was still somehow sexy. Every piece of it was form-fitting and showed off her beautiful curvy body. Her hair fell neatly over her shoulders without a single flyaway, or a bit of frizz. She approached the receptionist confidently. She stood tall and gave a friendly smile.

"I'm the new intern for Grace Patterson", Ella stated matter-of-factly. The receptionist pointed to a nearby seat and told her to wait till Grace came down to get her. Ella sat down and began flipping through a design book she had tucked neatly into her purse. Ella had been told to be here at eight in the morning, but it was almost nine before Grace made an appearance. She talked to the receptionist who gestured to Ella. Grace looked back at Ella with a displeased expression. She waved for Ella to follow her. Ella jumped up from the chair, remembering to maintain good posture as they walked down a long hallway, then up three flights of stairs, then halfway down the fourth-floor hallway and into a small office that opened to a larger one. Grace held her arms up when they entered the smaller office.

"This is your office, keep it tidy at all times, and no peanuts ever because I'm allergic", Miss Patterson demanded.

Ella peeked into Grace's office before sitting in her rolling computer chair in front of a desk that held a large Mac desktop computer. Moments later Grace had returned with a sheet of paper placing it on Ella's desk.

"These are your responsibilities for the day. Please try to get them all done", Grace said with a clipped tone.

Ella glanced over the list and it included creating some hard copy files, a few mailing and stuffing tasks, and a large report that she knew would take at least all day. She breathed a sigh of relief when Grace said she could take the report home. So, Ella got straight to work, and within twenty minutes she had the files printed and was organizing and stapling them as instructed. She then jotted down to the mailroom and it took her an hour to send out the items Grace needed sent. Once that was done Ella grabbed her lunch and returned to her desk. After she finished eating and cleaning up, she began the last, and most difficult task on the list. Which was typing out the report Grace had requested. By the end of the day, she was barely more than halfway through the report, so she gathered it together, put it neatly into her bag, and headed home to get it done.

The next day Ella dragged herself to work despite having been up all night finishing the report. Grace looked at her in disappointment without having so much as glanced at her work. The days were long and boring. She got similar lists each day and scrambled to get them done on time. As Ella walked across the hall and to the mail room she spotted a very handsome man and immediately wanted him. Suddenly Grace walked over and kissed the attractive man on his lips. Ella could not help but roll her eyes at the couples show of affection and sulk away to the mailroom. Before she closed the door behind her she looked back, and she swore she saw him staring at her as he remained in an embrace with her boss. He quickly moved his gaze, so it was difficult to tell whether he had been staring at her or not. Ella sat at her desk as Grace walked into the office with the man, who she introduced as her fiancé. She asked Ella to go get them both coffee from next door, so she did in a hurry so she could get back to working on the list. She brought the coffee back to the office, gave it to each of them and resumed her work. Ella had nearly passed right by the coffee shop as she walked home from work. When he waved at her, she stopped dead in her tracks. She was surprised to see that Grace's very handsome fiancé was waving her inside the coffee shop. She smiled at him and wondered what he needed from her as she walked inside the shop.

"What luck!", he exclaimed excitedly, "I'm Dimitri, you're my fiancée's assistant right?".

Ella silently nodded back at him with a curious expression.

"You somehow got my coffee order wrong. Do you remember exactly what you ordered?", he asked kindly.

Ella started to apologize but he cut her off. He said he liked it way better than how he normally ordered it and he and the barista had been trying to figure out what the difference was. Ella told him she got heavy cream instead of milk, and she explained that it was her usual drink, so she probably ordered it like that for him out of habit. Dimitri ordered two of them and invited Ella to sit down with him to drink her coffee. She knew she should not because of her unfinished work, but she took a seat across from him regardless. Ella took a sip of her drink and watched as Dimitri did the same. She sighed pleasantly and told Ella that he was glad she had messed his order up. He asked how long she had been interning for Grace. When Ella told him just a few days, he warned her that she could be difficult to work with. He just nodded as Ella assured him that she could handle it. She wondered what made Grace so bad when she saw the disbelief on his face. She thanked him for the coffee, and he offered her his business card.

"If you have any questions or need some advice", he offered kindly. She smiled and took the card from him. She tried to say thank you to him, but he insisted that it was him who should thank her.

When she resumed walking, she examined the business card. She gasped when she realized that he was a doctor. She decided that based on how successful he seemed, she was not incredibly surprised by that fact, as she tucked the card safely into her wallet. After walking only a block further, she was at her beautiful and historic, downtown apartment building. Ella went inside and worked until she fell fast asleep. She woke up to her alarm screaming at her. She jumped up and began quickly getting ready, trying to avoid being late. She cussed herself for falling asleep when she realized that she had not yet finished her report. When she made it to work, she already had coffee hoping it would cushion the blow Grace would almost certainly deal when she saw the unfinished report. Despite the coffee her heart still pounded when Grace finally made an appearance. Ella's gut feeling was right, Grace lost it, and for the rest of the day it seemed to be her mission to make Ella's life more difficult. She was constantly sending her to do gopher tasks, which halted her ability to complete her work. Ella held her frustrations inside as she endured the awful attitude Grace had towards her all day. The next couple days were no different either. So, on the fourth day she dialed Dimitri's number and asked if they could meet. He met her at the coffee shop an hour later and she immediately told him everything as tears welled up in her eyes.

He comforted her and told her he would meet with her later in the week with some completed reports he already had on hand that Ella could take the credit for. He also offered to walk her back to her apartment since it was dark outside. Ella graciously accepted both of his offers. They made small talk on the way back to her apartment. Ella wondered why Dimitri was being so kind to her, but she thought it might be rude to ask that question, so she did not. When they stood in front of her building, he offered her some comforting words and went in for a hug. Although it made her uncomfortable, because he was engaged to her boss, Ella did not want to appear rude, especially to someone who was trying to help her, so she returned his hug. When she did, he leaned in and kissed her on the lips. She looked at him stunned and tried to hide how pleased she was by it. As politely as she could, she asked Dimitri not to do that again. She explained that she did not want to risk her internship. Dimitri profusely apologized to Ella and said that he understood her situation. He asked if she would be kind enough to not say anything about it to Grace. Ella assured him that she had no plans to do that and then she turned and walked into her building without another word.

The next few days were more of the same. Grace piled on impossible workloads and every interaction between them was more unpleasant than the last. She sighed a huge sigh of relief when Dimitri texted her three days later. They agreed to meet again at the coffee shop. He handed her the reports and offered to buy her a coffee. She apologized and declined, saying that she had too much to do to be sitting in a coffee shop. She tucked the reports under her arm and excitedly made her way back to her apartment. Dimitri offered to walk her again, but she declined, simply stating that she did not want things with her boss to get any worse. So, Ella walked home alone and breathed a sigh of relief when she arrived safely home. Ella opened the door and immediately started to finish the necessary tasks. When she was done, she stacked the papers on the table where she would see them in the morning. She then went to bed and had vivid nightmares about losing her internship.

Ella woke up before her alarm began to buzz at her. She went ahead and set it off and started a pot of coffee. She took a shower and got herself ready for work. When the time came, she grabbed her bags and picked the stack of papers up off the table and made her way to work. Grace was fashionably late as usual.

She walked in and glared at Ella, "I hope you have your report done today", the snippiness in her voice infuriated Ella.

Regardless, Ella managed to plaster a fake smile on as she handed the stack of papers to Grace. She looked them over with a surprised expression but did not make any comments on them. Ella was fuming, but she kept her focus on her work and that helped her to refrain from reacting. Grace eased up on berating her for the day, but it almost infuriated her even more that Grace refused her any credit for handing in her report, plus two additional reports. She packed her stuff up and was getting ready to leave when Grace walked up with a page in her hand.

She laid the paper on her desk, "since I know you can handle the workload, I'd like this report handed in tomorrow as well", Grace's voice sounded cold and calculated.

Ella felt something in her snap, but she did not react in front of Grace. She waited until she had left the office and begun walking home. She pulled her phone out and dialed Dimitri's number. He answered on the second ring. She put on some tears that were only half-fake and told him all about how the mean bitch Grace had treated her at work today. He said he wanted to meet up with her, but this time they are going to get something a little stronger than coffee. When she walked up to the bar, he was already sitting at a table in the corner of the room.

She walked in and sat down next to Dimitri and looked at him with sad eyes. He placed his muscular arm around her shoulders and comforted her. She snuggled into the embrace secretly feeling delighted by what was happening. After a couple drinks, he predictably offered to escort her home, and she accepted his offer. When they got to the front of her apartment building, she noticed that he was shivering a little.

"Would you like to come up for a drink and to warm up? He said that he would be delighted to. She led him to the elevator and up to her apartment. Once they were both inside, she made a couple drinks. She sat on the couch next to him and he put his hand on her leg. She looked up at him and he made a second attempt at kissing her. This time she welcomed his kiss. She pressed her lips against his hard and they began to explore each other's bodies.

"Could I perhaps ask for a favor Ella?", he asked.

She said he could, so he explained that Grace flat out refuses to fulfill a long-time fantasy of his. He asked Ella if she might be willing to do it. She looked up at him curiously and asked what it was that he wanted. He told her he wanted to stick his cock in her ass. Anytime this had come up in the past it terrified her, but this time it turned her on. She agreed to do this for him, and they began removing each other's clothes. Once they both were naked, he grabbed Ella by the hips and bent her over the back to the couch. Her pussy got so wet he was able to use the juices as a lubricant for her tight little asshole. Ella remained perfectly still as Dimitri slowly worked his hard cock against her asshole until it began to let him in. She felt a searching pain as his cock stretched her virgin asshole. Once his cock was fully inside her, the pain began to slowly subside, and pleasure took its place. She moaned as his cock began to pound into that tight hole relentlessly. She moaned and wriggled against him as he thrusted into her. He had begun to groan. Sweat began dripping down their bodies and onto the couch and Dimitri's body began to clench up with pleasure. She felt him shake and strain as he began to speed up. He grabbed her hips and held on tight as he began to thrust and move his cock in and out of her ass. He stopped and let out a loud moan. His body clenched for a moment, but after a minute it was gone.

"Damn, I feel like I'm going to cum," he said. He pulled out of her ass and sat down on the couch. Ella slowly stood up, turned around, bent over and spread her ass cheeks. She pulled her ass cheeks apart and allowed

Dimitri to slip his fingers in between her butt cheeks. His fingers slowly began to explore her ass hole as she continued to allow her ass to be fucked by his finger. He pushed his cock into her pussy as he played with her ass until she moaned loudly and pleaded with him to fuck her ass. He slowly put another finger in her ass and pushed it in farther. His fingers felt so good Ella begged him to put his cock in her ass. Dimitri smiled and nodded. She nodded back and began to get nervous again. He pulled his cock out of her pussy and her asshole juices began to pulsate in anticipation. She gave a little cry as he started to slowly push in and out of her ass again. As his cock began to move back and forth in her ass, Ella moaned loudly and squeezed her butt cheeks. The pain was intense at first, but the more he moved it, the less it hurt. Once he was all the way inside her ass, she moaned loudly and pulled her ass cheeks apart. She was so turned on she began to push back against him.

"Oh god, it feels so good," she said. She began to rock back and forth slowly. Her fingers ran along her pussy as she pushed back at him. She wanted him to come soon so she could cum with him. He was shaking and holding on tight to her hips as he continued to slowly fuck her ass. He leaned back against the back of the couch and leaned his head against the cushions. Ella continued to push back against him as his cock moved in and out of her ass. Her whole body was shaking. She was so horny, her pussy was flooding with cum. Dimitri seemed close to coming too. Then just as she had anticipated she felt his body go tense again. His cock began to slowly pump his cum into her ass. She squeezed her ass cheeks together hard against him, trying to force as much as she could inside her.

She pulled away and grabbed his cock and started to give him a blowjob. She sucked him hard, pulling his cock all the way to the back of her mouth. She slowly let her lips wrap around the head of his cock, and slowly wrapped her mouth around his shaft. Her mouth was so hot and wet he was almost ready to explode. "Oh god," he said, as Ella sucked him hard. Ella pulled his cock out of her mouth and put her hand on his dick again. She stroked him slowly, pulling on his dick with her hand as she squeezed and pushed his cock back into her already jizz filled ass. He fucked her a moment longer before his alarm began buzzing. Alerting him that he had to get home. Dimitri gathered his stuff, put his clothes back on, and thanked Ella before saying goodbye to her. Ella felt satisfied by the night's events. She readied herself for bed not bothering to work on her reports. She wanted so bad to make sure that Grace would become aware of what happened between Dimitri and her. She wanted to gloat and make Grace feel as shitty as Grace had been causing her to feel at work, but she doubted she would go through with telling Grace anything about tonight for Dimitri's sake.

Ella pondered this before going to bed. The idea of quitting her internship also occurred to her. It was a very enticing idea because she did not know how much more of Grace's rude and demeaning behavior she could endure before she snapped. All that night, Ella dreamed of Dimitri and how sexy he was when he was fucking her asshole, and how good it felt to have her asshole fucked for the first time.

Ella finished her story by telling Dayna how she had quit the internship without explanation. Dayna looked at Ella nearly in shock. She was impressed by the actions Ella took in the story. She liked that Ella had refused to put up with Grace's bullshit.

"After knowing you in high school, I never would've guessed you would do something like that. I would expect something like that from me, but you? No way". Ella smiled and shrugged. They laughed for a moment about Ella's ballsy way of standing up to her tyrant of a boss. Ella's boob job was still relatively new, and her bra was getting increasingly uncomfortable as the night went on. She tried to adjust it so that it sat more comfortably but no matter what she did the wires pressed against her incisions causing her discomfort.

"I've got to go to the restroom and lose this thing", she said to Dayna as she pinched the top of her bra to show Dayna what she was talking about.

"I'll come with you if you don't mind", Dayna said as she stood up and walked across the bar and to the restroom with Ella. Once inside Ella stripped off her shirt and Dayna helped her undo the clasp that sat against her back. Ella slid the bra off her arms, dropped it into her purse, and began to massage the soreness out of her tender, swollen boobs.

"I wish I had some like that", Dayna said as she admired Ella's upgrade.

"Yours are perfect", Ella exclaimed. Dayna asked if she could feel Ella's boobs, just for research purposes of course. Ella said she could so Dayna cupped one in her hand and looked at Ella.

"Wow, they feel great", Dayna exclaimed.

Ella smiled, "I do love them. Do I get to feel yours now?", she joked.

"I guess so, if you want to", Dayna responded.

"Beautiful", Ella said as she cupped Dayna's boob in her hand," Your tits really do fit your body perfectly".

"Thanks", Dayna said. She was a little surprised when Ella actually reached over and grabbed her boob.

"You should go without a bra too, so I'm not the only one", Ella suggested. Dayna shrugged and removed her bra and put it into her purse. Both girls put their shirts back on and examined themselves in the mirror before returning to their table. The bartender brought them each a drink and said it was from the guy across the bar. The girls looked over and saw an older gentleman waving at them. Both girls waved back and yelled a thank you across the bar. They turned their attention back to one another. The man across the bar continued watching them as Dayna began her next story.

Three Is Better Than Two (Threesome)

Dayna had just woken up and looked at her clock. Still four hours till she had to be at the Cranmer's to watch their son Garret. The Cranmer's were a beautiful and wealthy couple. Arlene was tall and thin. She had long auburn hair that fell to the middle of her back. She looked ten years younger than she was. George was in shape and had a kind face. His salt and pepper hair gives it away that he is in his forties, but not much else about him does. They were heavily involved in the community and had college educations, and well-paying jobs. Their two-year-old son, Garret, was a bit rambunctious, but she did not complain. This job was a godsend. It came at a time when Dayna was on the verge of losing her home. Then she would have to move back in with her mom and Danny, and she did not want to do that with Brady. She got up and began pouring a bowl of cereal for her son. As she sat the bowl in front of him, she grabbed the toy truck he had carried to the table.

"You can have it back when you're finished with your breakfast", Dayna told him firmly.

"Awe, mommy", he whined as his shoulders slumped and he began to pout. Moments later he picked up his spoon and began eating anyway. Dayna watched him in adoration as he ate. His chubby little cheeks moved in and out as he chewed his cereal. He pushed the bowl away when he had finished and pointed to the truck sitting on the counter.

"Please", he said sweetly. Dayna helped him down from his seat before handing him the truck.

"Here you go", she said as she planted a kiss on the top of his head. He ran off to his room to play with the rest of his toys and Dayna sipped her coffee in peace. She opened the refrigerator and gazed inside. She could not find anything she wanted so she closed it and returned to her coffee after jotting a few items on her grocery list.

Dayna began getting herself ready while Brady was in his room playing. He must have heard the water start running because she heard his little footsteps coming quickly down the hall. He told her he wanted to brush his teeth with her, so she squeezed a dot of bubblegum-flavored toothpaste onto his spider-man toothbrush and handed it to him. He vigorously scrubbed his teeth. She had to lift him up to the sink so that he could spit and rinse. She carefully selected an outfit for him. The Cranmer's son Garret was always so well-dressed. You would never see a single stain on his clothes, nor any worn knees. Dayna tried to ensure Brady was well-dressed when they went over there too, because she did not want the Cranmer's to think badly of her. Dayna cared very much about the impression she gave the Cranmer's. They were so well put together. She was careful to always be on time and to present herself well, especially since they had been helping her out so much.

She finished getting herself and her son ready and she began packing his diaper bag with all the necessities she thought she might need for him. She loaded everything into the car and stopped along the way to get the boys some bath paints to play with during their bath that evening. Dayna arrived at the Cranmer's house about thirty minutes early. She got out of the car and walked around to unbuckle Brady. He was already yelling Garret's name loudly and looking at the house impatiently waiting to see his best friend. Dayna smiled, thinking about how adorable their friendship is and how quickly they had formed such a strong bond. Brady was a shy kid, but he took to Garret right away, and they have been inseparable ever since. Dayna lifted Brady onto her hip as he tried to struggle out of her arms so that he could run to knock on the door himself. Dayna asked him to stop and assured him that he could play with his friend very soon. Brady took on an expression that indicated he was thinking about it before he decided to calm down.

Dayna lightly knocked at the door. She heard a shuffle from the inside of the house and then she heard Garrett yelling at the door before George opened the door. He had on his black slacks and no shirt or shoes. There was dew on his skin suggesting he had recently gotten out of the shower. Dayna could not help but notice how great his body was for an older man. His lower stomach had that sexy v shape right above where his pants sat on his hips. Dayna pulled her attention away from George's body. She did not want to be caught staring at him like that. The last thing she wanted to do was disrespect Arlene, who had been so kind to her. George smiled at her knowingly, which alarmed Dayna at first, but she convinced herself that he had not seen her gawking and tried to pretend nothing had happened.

"Hey babe, Dayna's here", he called up to Arlene. Moments later she came down the stairs as she was trying to put an earring in her ear. She finally got it through and put the clasp on the back, then she hugged Dayna tight.

She wore a stunning full-length gown. Much of the back was cut out exposing her bare skin which was beautifully pale. Her red hair fell over her shoulders, complementing the green dress. Dayna caught herself gawking at Arlene too, but that was not nearly as offensive, she decided.

"You look stunning", Dayna said to her, sounding in awe. Arlene smiled and looked down at herself and then backed up to meet Dayna's eye.

"Do you think so?", she questioned. Dayna nodded in approval.

"That's my beautiful wife", George said as he walked up. Once he was close, he slipped his hand around her waist and pulled her in for a kiss. She put her hand on his chest and pushed him back as she looked him up and down.

"Go finish getting ready", she demanded pointing towards their room, "We don't have much time before the party starts". George frowned and began to make his way back up the stairs. Arlene turned to Dayna and pulled a necklace from a small box. "Could I get your help?", Arlene asked sweetly.

"Of course,", Dayna said as she carefully took the necklace from Arlene, who turned her back to Dayna. As Dayna looped the necklace around Arlene's throat, she noticed how beautiful the silver and shining red gems looked against her skin. "What kind of party are you attending?", Dayna asked curiously. Arlene lowered her voice to a whisper.

"Between you and me", she began, "George and I concluded that our life in the bedroom was going dull. So, a friend invited us to go to a swinger's ball". Dayna's mouth gaped open. She had never imagined that the Cranmer's would go to a swinger's ball. Arlene giggled at the expression on Dayna's face. Dayna fumbled for an apology, but Arlene shushed her.

"No big deal", she said waving her hand, "Truthfully I'm as shocked as you are". Arlene began telling Dayna that Garret had been very hyper over the past few days. Dayna tried to listen, but she could not get over what she had just heard, so she just nodded, only really hearing some of what Arlene was saying. Dayna snapped out of her daze when George reappeared beside them. He looked very handsome in his button up shirt and slacks. His tie lay around his neck waiting to be tied. Arlene took the two ends of the tie in her hands and gracefully tied it. They both looked flawless. You would think they were going to something much more official than a swinger's party. Dayna still could not wrap her mind around it, but she wished the Cranmer's a wonderful night, and said goodbye to them as they walked out to their car.

Dayna called out for the boys wondering where they were. She checked the living room to see if they were watching television, but they were not there. She made her way slowly up the stairs and to the playroom where all Garret's toys were. Then she heard squeals coming from across the hall where Garret's room was. The boys were jumping up and down on the bed. Dayna called out for them. They both stopped jumping and turned to look at her with curiosity on their faces. She politely asked them not to do that anymore. She warned them that one of them could get seriously hurt. Both boys got down from the bed without another word. Dayna sent them off to the playroom to play with Garrett's toys, and she went to the kitchen to figure out what she was going to make for dinner. She was rooting around in the kitchen when she heard a knock at the door. Dayna looked out the peephole and saw a bright red hat. She curiously opened the door and there stood a young man. He was wearing a uniform with a pizza shaped logo and holding a box. Dayna took the pizza figuring that the Cranmer's probably ordered it for her and the boys. Arlene probably told her that she was going to order pizza, but Dayna had been so shocked by the bit of information she learned about the couple, that she probably did not hear it.

"Boys, Pizza!", she yelled up the stairway loudly hoping they would hear her over their playing. A few moments later she heard little footsteps thumping down the hallway and Garrett yelling about pizza enthusiastically. She grabbed two plates out of the cabinet and turned around to both boys staring at her expectantly wearing huge grins. Dayna smiled and put a piece of pepperoni pizza on each of their plates and sat both plates on the table. Garrett climbed into his chair with ease as she lifted Brady into his. They both finished their pieces leaving only the crust behind. Dayna offered them a second slice but both boys were ready to get back to playing. While they did Dayna sat down on the couch to check her phone and let the Cranmer's know how the evening was going so far. Arlene responded with a thumbs up. Dayna got lost in thought about what the ball must be like. Mostly naked people all over the place. People fucking in every corner of the room. On couches and beds, sex swings hanging from the ceilings. Arlene being fucked by a stranger, and George fucking a stranger.

Dayna noticed her pussy was getting wet. She felt the need to get off, badly. She did not much care for using just her fingers, so she snuck into the Cranmer's room promising herself she would leave no evidence of her intrusion. Once inside their room she searched under the bed, there was nothing there but some boxes full of old keepsakes. She then looked in the nightstand drawer and again found nothing of interest. She pressed down on the clothes in the dresser, feeling for anything that was not clothes. She felt something firm and long, so she carefully lifted the clothes and there lay a purple vibrator. She smiled and picked it up. Before laying down on their bed she twisted the bottom of the vibrator. It came to life, buzzing hard in her hand. She was surprised by how much power the thing had. Her pussy got even more wet as she anticipated feeling it on and in her eager pussy. Dayna removed her pants and carefully laid them on the dresser. Dayna laid back on their bed and spread her legs open readying herself.

Dayna pushed the lace of her thong to the side and touched her throbbing clit with the tip of her finger. She twirled her finger in a circular motion a few times before picking up the vibrator that lay buzzing on the bed beside her. She slowly brought it to her clit and touched it lightly. Her body jumped in response to the intense pleasure that immediately coursed through her. She took a deep breath and then slid the toy as far into her mouth as she could. When she pulled it out, she tried to leave ample spit to use as lubricant. She put the toy over her tight little hole and slowly pushed it inside. She pulled it in and back out a few times and then she swirled it around inside her pussy. As she slid it out this time, she pulled it up towards her stomach letting the tip stop on her clit. She began to move it in a slow circular motion. Her body began to shake, and she felt the orgasm welling up inside her. She willed it to come, and then it did. She arched her back and moaned as pleasure took over her mind, every part of her body tensed up and then fell limp when it was over. She lay there for a few moments longer to catch her breath. Then she got up from the bed and went to the bathroom to wash her juices off the toy. She returned the vibrator to its spot and looked over the room once more before walking out and closing the door behind her.

Dayna went upstairs and into the bathroom to fill the bathtub for the boys. When the tub was full, she opened the bath paint she had bought and yelled for the boys. They followed her voice to the bathroom and when they saw the full tub and the paints they were excited to get in. She washed them up and let them play for a short while before taking them out, drying them, and getting them into their pajamas. They were reluctant to lay down, so she bribed them with a story. Even after the story, they both had to be reminded multiple times that it was bedtime. Dayna had just got both boys to fall asleep. They had put up quite a fight this evening. As Arlene had warned, Garrett had been especially rambunctious today, but Dayna could not complain, Garret gave her little man a friend to play with, plus she was incredibly lucky to have gotten this job. Without it there is no way she would be able to get her bills paid. She sat on the couch and began mindlessly flipping through the channels.

Suddenly, Dayna heard the Cranmer's laughing outside the door as they came in. It sounded like they had a pleasant time. She greeted them when they walked in and then started gathering Brady's things and grabbed the car keys from her purse so she could unlock her car, set her things inside, and carry Brady out. She smiled and asked how their night had gone, they said it went well. Dayna noticed a slight slur in their voices which was likely due to alcohol. They had been drinking, which was generally good for Dayna because they tipped her more generously when they are intoxicated. Dayna told the couple about how the boys played together non-stop and that she did not have much of a problem out of them. The couple thanked her and as Dayna had predicted, they handed her an envelope with seventy-five dollars in it. Dayna thanked them and wished them a good night as she walked back to the room where the boys slept so she could grab Brady. She lifted him onto her hip with his head laying on her shoulder. She froze momentarily to let him drift back into a deep sleep. Then she carefully carried him out to her car. She secured her son into his car seat and walked around to the driver's side and got into the car. She let the defrost run for a moment before she pulled out of the driveway. A few minutes later she pulled into her driveway and carried Brady inside. She laid him in her bed and cuddled up next to him and went to sleep.

She felt her phone buzzing beneath her. When she cracked her eyes open, she saw the sun streaming in through the window and Brady staring down at her as he waited patiently beside her. He complained that he was hungry, so Dayna got up and fixed him a bowl of cereal. He sat and ate his food without a single complaint. As she drank her coffee Dayna checked her phone. There was a text from the Cranmer's. They wanted her to watch Garrett again tonight. Dayna figured something unexpected must have come up. They promised to pay her extra if she babysits tonight. She texted them back saying that she would be happy to, but she reminded them that her mom always got Brady on Saturday, so it would just be her coming this time. They said that was fine and asked her to be there at seven, which was much later than normal. Dayna spent the day hanging out and playing with Brady. Then at six she dropped him off to her mom and went straight to the Cranmer's house. She arrived about fifteen minutes early and tapped lightly on the door. Arlene answered the door wearing nothing but a robe. Dayna figured she was probably running behind on getting ready. She greeted Arlene quickly, and then tried to give her space to get ready. She looked around and did not see nor hear Garret, so she asked where he was.

"He's at my sister's house this evening actually", Arlene said coolly. Dayna looked at her quizzically. If Garrett is at Arlene's sisters, why on earth was she here? Just then George walked down the steps, and much like Arlene, he was wearing nothing but a gray pair of sweatpants. Dayna was getting increasingly confused by everything that was happening.

"Oh, hey Dayna, you made it!", George said casually as he walked past the ladies and into his room.

Once he was out of earshot, Arlene leaned in close to Dayna as if to tell her a secret, "I absolutely must tell you about how our evening went", her breath smelled of something sweet with a hint of booze. Arlene told Dayna that despite their efforts they did not make many friends at the swinger's ball it was not that people did not like them. Plenty of men and women made passes at the couple. Unfortunately, everyone there was older, and they were hoping to meet someone young, sweet, and ripe. Dayna listened intently as she tried to figure out why she was here. Just then George came in carrying three champagne flutes. Arlene took two from him and passed one over to Dayna as he sat down. She took a big gulp to quench her thirst.

George looked at her with a look of disapproval on his face. "You know, I'm very disappointed in you Dayna", he began.

Dayna was so confused. She fiddled her thumbs as she waited for an explanation. Suddenly the realization hit her. She decided that she would just deny any wrongdoing. There is no way they possibly could know about her sneaky trip into their room for certain. She must have left some evidence behind but as she thought it over, she became convinced that there was no way they could possibly know for certain what happened in that room. He looked at her suspiciously as if waiting for her to confess, she could feel the pressure, but she remained silent and took another gulp of her mimosa. Arlene chimed in without warning,

"We never would've noticed if it had not been for the cum you left behind on our bed", she said thoughtfully. She leaned over to put her hand on Dayna's thigh. She said she was not mad at all and told Dayna that it was okay. Dayna worried about losing her job babysitting for them. She needed the money so badly. Arlene sat back up and finished her mimosa.

"I mean, at least she cleaned my toy off afterwards, right honey?", she said turning to George.

Dayna wondered how in the world they knew that. George's expression hardened, "What pisses me off is that she did not include us, and she did it in our home".

Arlene touched his shoulder, "At least we got to enjoy the footage though, right babe?".

Dayna's heart nearly stopped, "footage?", she whimpered quietly. The reality struck her that they must have had hidden security cameras in their room. Tears welled up in her eyes.

"Don't fret dear", Arlene said compassionately, "It was really great footage", she suggested as if it were supposed to make Dayna feel better. George suggested that they let her watch it. They ushered her upstairs and into his office. He started up his computer and opened his files and clicked on one with yesterday's date on it. After fast forwarding for a moment Dayna came into the frame. They all sat and watched as she used Arlene's toy in their bed. When the footage was over George seemed to be fuming even more.

"You can make it up to us can't you sweety?" she said, turning to Dayna. Dayna was unsure exactly what she meant. How was she supposed to make it up to them? The realization suddenly hit her. She remembered George's comment earlier about not including them and everything clicked into place.

"It would save your job", Arlene suggested with a soft voice.

They wanted her to have sex with them. She thought about George's knowing expression after he caught her checking him out and Arlene saying that they did not have success at the swinger's ball because they wanted someone younger.

She looked at them both, and tried to choose her words carefully, "I just really don't want to cause any problems between the two of you, or have things be awkward".

Arlene busted out laughing. She insisted that their relationship was solid and could withstand this, and in fact needed it. "Besides", she chimed in with a seductive voice, "we are all adults here, there is no reason we should not be able to have a little fun without it becoming awkward or any jealous feelings, right?". Dayna pondered the idea in her mind. She thought about the job and how much she needed it. Arlene had said this would save her job, and she would do anything for her son. Not that she was not already attracted to both George and Arlene.

Just then as if Arlene had been reading her mind, she set an envelope on the table, "Plus there's this in it for you". Dayna eyed the envelope and Arlene gestured for her to pick it up. She carefully lifted it from the table and peered inside. She flipped through the bills inside counting it up. Her eyes widened when she counted the sum of the money in the envelope. A thousand dollars in hundred-dollar bills were contained in the envelope. She knew she had to do it. That was a lot of money and the alternative was losing her job.

She nodded at the couple and told them that she would like to make it up to them.

Arlene smiled as if she had known this would be the result, and George's expression softened, "Really?", he said in disbelief. When they first texted her asking her to work another evening, they had already informed Dayna that this noteworthy babysitting job would be an overnight one, and they intended to keep that promise. In addition, Arlene had already planned everything meticulously, and there were to be some surprises for Dayna throughout the evening. Arlene told Dayna that she would be receiving some instructions from her over the intercom system, which she had no idea they had. She was told to go to their bedroom, shower and ready herself for the evening as quickly as possible and wait for their instructions. She did as she was told and made her way to their bedroom. To Dayna's surprise, Arlene had the foresight to leave two gifts that were both thoughtful, and appropriate waiting for her on the bed. The first was a clearly expensive romper with a silky, purple fabric that was transparent, and was trimmed with intricate black lace.

Dayna put it on and marveled at the way she looked and felt in it. The fabric felt soft and silky against her skin. Her puckered nipples were clearly visible, in fact every part of her body was visible through the fabric. It looked great on her and she felt so luxurious in it. The second gift was a twin to Arlene's powerful purple vibrator she had used, she guessed the Cranmer's got it because they had been able to tell in the security footage exactly how much she had enjoyed it. Arlene's voice came through the intercom instructing her to use the gifts that she left. She told her to have the romper on and be in the bed using the vibrator that Arlene had gifted her. Not long after she heard the door open and the couple came into the room. Dayna was there, and in the four-poster bed, writhing with pleasure from the intense vibrations of her new toy. Without hesitation, they took the vibrator out of her hands right before she could reach her climax. They cuffed her hands together and then bound her cuffed hands to the bed. Then they restrained her legs and ankles to the bed as well, and she was lying flat on her back, but unable to move about freely. She was completely at their mercy.

"Oh, please put it back", she pleaded, "I was just about to come".

"I wanted to be the one to make you come. I am not going to let a vibrator do it", George declared.

"But…", Dayna whined.

"Honey if you beg, he's just going to make you wait longer", Arlene suggested with a sigh. Then Dayna clamped her mouth shut and tried to wait patiently. After getting so close, she had a tremendous desire to reach her climax and it was nearly driving her insane. The Cranmers started kissing and feeling against one another and ignoring her. Dayna could not help but to moan in frustration, wishing that they would caress her, touch her, feel her already wet pussy, and please her. Arlene walked over and eyed her for a moment with an expression of approval, then she rewarded Dayna by licking, sucking and nibbling her pussy. They both moaned with pleasure, and George walked over with his cock in hand, and stood at the head of the bed close to Dayna. She was just close enough to reach his cock, so she took it into her mouth and began to suck it. After a moment, his wife grabbed his arm and pulled him over where she was and he tasted Dayna's young wet pussy, and after just a few licks, Dayna's body tensed, and her pussy got even more wet as she came for him. His cock was throbbing, but he wanted to see his wife's face and tongue pleasing their babysitter's pussy and watch her taste the juices from the pleasure he had just given her. He pushed his wife's face hard into Dayna's pussy, getting even more turned on as they both moaned in response to the ecstasy they felt. He gave Dayna a slap on her thigh, remarkably close to her pussy, but without giving any direct stimulation. She begged him for more. He took a feather off a dream catcher that hung on the wall and trailed in up and down Dayna's body. He smacked her tits hard. He appreciated their perkiness, the benefit of having smaller boobs. The impact made her inhale in surprise at the first slap but soon she was enjoying the attention that her boobs were getting.

She began screaming and begging him for more. George lifted her ass up off the bed and signaled for Arlene to spank her ass. Arlene delivered blow after blow until Dayna's ass was warm and red. He asked his wife to sit on Dayna's face. Dayna tasted Arlene's sweet pussy. As George watched, he decided it was time to get his dick wet. He slid his rock-hard cock into her young, tight, pussy as she groaned and tried to thrust her pussy up into him. He moved his wife to the side to slap her in the face and told her that he would fuck her at his pace, not hers. She moaned and nodded in agreement. Then he told his wife to get on all fours so he could taste her pussy. Arlene's pussy was getting wetter. He could not remember ever feeling his wife's pussy so wet and she was getting ready to cum. Her juices rushed out of her pussy with a gush. She leaned over Dayna so she could taste her cum. She moaned loudly in appreciation and swallowed as much of it as she could . He placed a strap-on around Arlene's waist so he could watch her fuck Dayna. As the dildo entered their babysitter, she squirmed in pleasure. He liked the sight of his wife fucking her. He put his hands around Dayna's neck and lightly choked her to quiet her down. She enjoyed the punishment and groaned and smiled up at him as he varied the pressure on her throat.

He leaned down to taste her little pussy. His lips trailed kisses across her body, from her neck down her chest he was giving each nipple some attention and continued kissing her till he reached her stomach. His wife stopped fucking her so he could place his tongue on Dayna's.
wet, waiting pussy, and instantly she came, splashing his face with her sweet juice. He licked up all the cum he could as she squirmed against his tongue. He began to feel an intense need to fuck them both. He placed his wife on all fours directly over Dayna so that their holes are both within his cock's reach. He began fucking them both alternating from one to the other at his will. He spread his wife's lips and thrust himself inside fast and hard. She was unbelievably wet, and he slid in and out of her with ease.

He looked up to see the women kissing each other intimately and went at his wife harder and faster. Dayna began begging to be fucked. He pulled out of Arlene, and spread Dayna's ass to force his thick, rock hard cock into her tight little asshole. He thrusted hard and fast into her as both his wife and Dayna moaned in pleasure. Dayna began to beg for his cum. He hesitated for a moment until Arlene told him to cum inside her ass. Then he lost all the control he had left and spurted his cum deep inside of her and kept thrusting until every drop was inside her. As he pulled out his cock the cum came dripping out of her ass. Arlene put her mouth underneath and began to catch the cum with her mouth. Dayna lay there panting as they untied her. She felt so satisfied that she made sure to inform them that she would be more than happy to do this again whenever they wanted.

Ella fought the urge to start rubbing her pussy right there in the bar. Dayna's story had her so worked up that she was dying for some cock right about now.

"You got to live one of those fantasies that everyone wishes they could", she looked at Dayna and smiled, "You don't happen to still have their contact information, do you?", she said jokingly. Both girls broke into a fit of laughter.

Dayna told Ella it had been years since she had heard from them, "but I bet they're still freaks", she said with a huge grin. She told Ella how they had helped her discover her fetish for authority figures. She had many more similar rendezvous with them afterwards. It became a routine up until she had saved up the money and bought a house. Her new home unfortunately was too far away for her to continue babysitting for them, and then they just lost contact with each other. Afterwards she craved and sought out similar experiences. She liked being roughed up like that. The loss of control was such a big turn on. Ella nodded in agreement. She herself had experienced a lot of that, and it seems to never lose its appeal.

By this point both girls had consumed more drinks than they probably should've, and they were quite intoxicated. The slurs in their voices were becoming increasingly noticeable and they were now telling their stories without any hesitations. They openly shared all the freakiest details of their sex lives. They considered the fact that they both had far drives to get home, or in Ella's case, to her hotel. They decided to quit drinking and place an order for some food. They agreed they did not want to spend a night in jail or worse, so they began to try to sober up to safely get themselves where they needed to go. They looked over the menu again before ordering sandwiches, because they figured the bread might help soak up some of the alcohol. Dayna suggested Ella tell another story as they wait for their food to arrive. Ella already had the perfect story in mind. This one happened sometime after she had finished her internship, which she ended up not doing with Grace of course. In fact, after sleeping with Dimitri, Ella did not return to her internship with Grace. She had gotten fed up with being treated that way. Before Ella began her story, she checked her phone and gasped. To her surprise, her hotel reservation had been canceled earlier in the evening. Dayna mentioned that there was a decent hotel nearby, so Ella quickly placed a reservation before jumping into her story.

Ella's Master (BDSM)

Ella was having a calm evening at home alone. She was watching Netflix on her couch with a bowl of popcorn in her lap, a glass of wine in her hand, and a throw blanket laying across her bare legs. She was home alone so she had on just a t-shirt, and a thong. It had been an incredibly long week. Ella had just finished her internship and was about to begin searching for a full-time position on a good design team. She had a few places in mind that she knew had positions available, but she still needed to update her resume before she could submit it, and first she just wanted to take a few days to relax and celebrate. She felt she deserved it after a full academic year spent as an intern, being underpaid and overworked. She lifted her glass to her wine-stained lips and took a slow sip. The horror movie she was watching had her full attention. When the possessed doll popped out of the darkness she jumped and let out a small squeal. When she heard a clang, her attention turned curiously to the door that led to the basement in her adorable, historic, downtown home. Her heartbeat sped up, and she paused the movie and listened intently. After a few moments of complete silence, except the low hum of her air conditioning, she pressed play on the remote and began watching the movie again.

Ella supposed she was just a bit shook up. It should not come as a surprise considering everything that was going on in her life. She was asked to volunteer at a haunted house this year by helping design it. Also, she had just had to cut things off with the sugar daddy she has had since college because he was getting a little more serious than she wanted to be. At the haunted house, she was also playing a victim, who would be chained up to the ceiling by her arms, her white gown covered in blood, with fake intestines looking as if they were spilling out of her abdomen as she desperately screams for the spectators to help her. She had been at rehearsals all week. She met this hot guy there too. He was a little older, in his thirties, she assumed. He has asked her out and he is supposed to take her to a cool restaurant that is apparently doing a Halloween theme. He said it was supposed to be like eating in a haunted house. It sounded fun to Ella and she could not wait. They were even planning to wear their haunted house get up to dinner. By the time the movie had ended she had finished off five glasses of wine and was quite intoxicated. She made her way up the stairs and into her bedroom. She threw herself into bed and let the wine take her into a deep sleep.

Considering she had to get her costume for the haunted house on for the date, Ella began getting ready at around three in the afternoon. She got into the shower with the water running as hot as she could stand it. Her smooth skin began turning a bright red as the water ran down her body. She washed and rinsed her hair. She stepped out of the shower and onto the bathmat. Gathering all her hair up into her hands, she began to wring her hair out onto the bathmat, and then she wrapped a towel around her naked, red, and wet body. As she stood in front of the mirror, she used the towels to dry each part of her body before proceeding to blow dry her hair. When it was dry, she began to tease her hair and applied hairspray until it was a complete mess, like the hair of someone who had survived to the end of a horror movie should be. She sprayed even more hairspray until she was convinced that her hair would remain this way throughout the evening.

Next Ella began her makeup. She carefully placed various cuts and bruises at random places all over the parts of her body that would be visible in the thigh length white blood-stained gown. She paid special attention to the details in her face. She painted on dark sleepless eyes and some very convincing bloody wounds. She wondered if Evan was planning to go all out with it like she was doing. He seems enthusiastic about Halloween. Halloween was Ella's favorite holiday. She loved dressing up and scaring the shit out of people. After doing her makeup, she applied some finishing products to make her costume last. Once it dried, she carefully pulled her gown over her head. It fit snugly on her hips and chest, and the gown showed most of her legs as it barely covered her ass. She loved how sexy she looked in it even though she appeared to be nearly dead. She affixed her fake intestines to the front of her gown so that they appeared to be falling out of her with terrific gore.

When Ella finished getting ready, she poured herself a last-minute glass of wine and gulped it down and sprayed herself down with some perfume before doing one last costume check before she left. She smiled at her reflection in the mirror. She was thrilled with not only how terrifyingly realistic it all looked, but also how surprisingly sexy it was. The dress showed the perfect shape of her ass and left most of her legs exposed. She grabbed her purse off the back of a chair at her kitchen table, and then picked her keys up off the coffee table. She was careful to lock the doors before leaving. October always seemed to bring out people's crazy sides, especially in the city. She drove her car to a park near the restaurant where she had planned to meet up with Evan. She parked, got out of her car, and walked over to the restaurant to wait. Her date arrived looking dapper and terrifying. His costume makeup was every bit as good as hers.

They walked down the road in silence. Evan always seemed to have a quiet personality which made him mysterious. They walked up to an old and abandoned-looking building. It had a great ambiance thanks to great lighting and realistic decorations that convincingly made the place look and feel like a haunted house. Ella walked inside with her arm wrapped around Evan's. A creepy doorman with his head in the palm of his hand let them inside. A hostess who was decked out in gothic attire, complete with black nails and lips asked them if they have reservations. Evan pulled a card from his pocket and handed it to her. She glanced at it and nodded before leading them through the various terrifying scenes and to their table. Each table was sectioned off from the next for privacy. Every now and then, she would hear someone let out a blood curdling scream. On the walls next to them there were creepy animatronic hands everywhere. Occasionally, a few of them would move, scaring Ella and occasionally Evan. A zombie waitress came by to take their drink order.

She assured them she would be back with their beverages and disappeared back into the scene. A few minutes later she appeared with glasses full of a liquid that appeared to be blood but smelled like fruit punch and vodka. She ordered a mummified calzone and he asked for the monster BBQ chicken sliders. The food was simple but well prepared and arranged to look very suited for Halloween. More jump scares continued to surprise them all throughout the duration of dinner. Evan gave the waitress his card the moment she appeared with the bill. After they gulped down the last of their drink they stood to leave. Ella was grateful that Evan treated her to such a rare and cool experience. She was really enjoying herself. After leaving the restaurant the pair walked down the road together. The restaurant where they had eaten was not far from the location of the haunted house they were going to be volunteering at. When they approached it, Ella began to wonder how they were going to get it ready to open in time. The place was cluttered with various Halloween decorations. Evan wiggled the doorknob and the door easily came open. He looked back at Ella mischievously as he walked into the building. It was dark and cluttered inside. Evan turned his phone's flashlight on and shined it around the room. There were chains and hooks hanging from the ceiling and various decorations all over the floor.

Ella looked at Evan and had a very naughty thought. She walked over to him and dropped down to her knees. First Evan looked confused but as Ella began to unbutton his jeans, a look of realization crossed his face. Ella grabbed his cock and put it into her mouth. She sucked on it for a moment before the door busted open. Ella and Evan both nearly jumped out of their skin. A tall man with a mask came in.

"Ella, how could you do this to me?", he screamed. Ella was confused and shocked, so she just stood there wide-eyed. Evan looked at her in an accusatory way.

"You have a boyfriend?", he stated furiously. He left the building without another word. Once he was gone, the man laughed and walked over to her.

"Who are you?", Ella asked. He answered with a single word, Master. He grabbed her by the wrists and brought her to an area where chains were hanging from the ceiling. He chained her up by her wrists and lifted her dress. He ripped her panties off her. When he touched her pussy, he chuckled. She had not been able to help but get wet. She wished it did not but this whole scenario turned her on immensely. He heard him fumbling with his jeans for a moment before he began pounding into her pussy. As he did, he pinched her nipples so hard tears fell from her eyes. When he was finished, he declared himself her master, and informed her that her training was to begin soon. He left and she went to her car, looking over her shoulder the whole way. Part of her was excited about the upcoming "training", part of her was terrified.

Ella woke with a fear of Master and his punishment in the back of her mind, each morning she felt a mix of relief and disappointment that Master had not begun her training. Tonight, she hoped to put it out of her mind and relax with a bottle of bubbly in front of the giant 90-inch television she was gifted by her most recent sugar daddy. She wondered if she would ever be able to have another as the new man in her life had made it noticeably clear that he did not approve when he found her sucking Evan off in the haunted house. He ran Evan off and took her for himself, several times. He scared her, He had on that day told her that he claimed ownership over her, that he was her master now. He assured her that she should anticipate her forthcoming training. He would be in touch, he said. So, she waited.

"Why don't I go to the police?" she asked herself, many times these last few nights. He scared the shit out of her. But she was compelled to wait for him. Just as he commanded. Because he also created feelings which, as hard as she might try to put into words, she could not help but dream about. Not nightmares, no. These were a different kind of dreams. They were strangely realistic. She almost believed they had happened. Master stood over her as she woke, a sadistic grin on his face. She nearly screamed in horror.

"You start today, slut." Wordlessly, she nodded and got out of the bed. Master began to issue one-word utterances with slight motions of the wrist. "Strip." Briefly, the thought of an orchestrator directing his symphony passed through Ella's mind. When she would think back on it, he was more like a Necromancer. A ballet of pain and pleasure. A dance with the devil. "Now." And she did, all the way down to her underwear. He shook his head. With a sigh of reluctance, she took off the panties she wore during the night. He suddenly scooped her up in his arms around her waist and he began moving with haste. Before she knew it, she was thrown into the trunk of a car, her hands and feet were swiftly hogtied behind her back and the panties she had just dropped moments before, were shoved into her mouth. The Master stood there for a moment with a smug grin underneath the Halloween mask he wore. Then he slammed the trunk closed with Ella inside. A while later the trunk opened, and he untied her hands and feet. "Follow", he commanded. She followed him to the garage in his home. Yesterday, it had been filled with useless junk and odd broken Halloween props, today it was filled with Ella's nightmares. Rope, handcuffs, racks, gags, all types of machines and toys that half of which she did not even know what they could be for. Ella was terrified. Without a word, and with no compassion displayed, Master roughly grabbed Ella by the hair and pulled her over to an X-shaped cross. He pulled her legs apart, attaching them to the legs of the cross, and doing the same with her arms. Once Ella was sufficiently restrained, Master spoke.

"You know why you're here. You know what you have done. This is your punishment. Your training will turn you into my personal slave, my personal slut. Made to do exactly whatever I would have you do. Because after your little stunt, that is what you deserve my whore", he smiled at her as he spoke. Ella was stunned and bewildered. She could not believe the man had such disregard for the laws of man and god. She had no idea what he referred to. She had done lots of things but none that should have offended this stranger. "From this moment onwards, you will only refer to me as 'Master', and anyone else I decide to bring around you will be 'Master' or 'Mistress'. Am I understood?", he said expectantly.

Ella finally was able to break through her shock enough to speak. "Wait, who are you? What do you mean?! I did not do anything to you!", she screamed.

"You do not have a say in the matter. Everything you do now is to serve me. I will not hear another word out of you unless I ask for it. Am I understood?" Master viciously declared. Ella mutely nodded her head in defeat. He started preparing for the first task. He brought out a box of clothes pins. Ella looked at them with a mixture of fear and curiosity.

"I am going to attach 60 clothes pegs to various points on your body. Some painfully sensitive, some not so much. I am also going to attach a powerful vibrator to your leg and your cunt. For every minute you manage not to orgasm, that is another peg I will not pull off your little body. You last the whole hour, no pain. You last 15 minutes, that is 45 clothes pins that will get yanked from your body. Is the game understood?", as he spoke, he counted out the pins.

Ella responded with a simple, "Yes Master". She realized there was no way out of this situation except master's way. He just grinned, and she shivered at how evil he appeared. He pulled out the first pin, with a glint in his eye. He pinched some of the flesh around Ella's breast, pulled it taut and applied the peg. She yelped out in pain, "Ow!! That really hurts, stop!" Ella complained. He simply smiled at her pain.

"Good.", he said repeating the process, applying clothes pins to all her sensitive areas, her breasts, her abdominal area, her arms, and especially her pussy, each time eliciting a moan, a yelp, or a cry of pain from her. Once the process was completed, she was nearly on the verge of tears. Those tears brought her Master joy. He pulled out a vibrating wand which he was going to use on her. He tied it to her leg tightly and switched it on to its highest vibration setting. From the second Ella felt the sensations touch her pussy, she was moaning like a whore. Master was kind enough to remind her a couple times not to cum. She tried, desperately to hold her pleasure in, but eventually, around the 23-minute mark, she could not do it anymore, and she came with a lustful scream. A warm gush flowed down in between her legs.

"23 minutes. Not bad. You will have to improve of course. However, you still must deal with the penalty of disobedience", Master coldly remarked. Ella, with intense lust and fear in her eyes shook her head rapidly, begging him not to hurt her anymore.

She had tears streaming from her eyes as he continued to speak, "I know, my slave. I do not need to hurt you. I simply want to. And as I am your master, I reserve the right to do as I wish with you. You are now my property, and I will treat you as I wish", and with that, Master yanked off the first of the 37 pegs from her nipple. She screamed in pain, pleading with him to end her torment.

He looked at her coldly and pulled them off one by one. He yanked them from her breasts, her nipples, her pussy, and everywhere else, until there were only 23 left on her body. These Masters took off very carefully, as promised to cause her minimal pain. Through the entire ordeal, he had very much enjoyed delivering her pain, so that by the end of it she was crying like a newborn child. Master took her down from the cross and asked her one simple question. "Who are you?", he said looking at her curiously.

"I am your slave, M-Master", she replied through sobs and tears.

"Brilliant. Now prove it. Suck me dry slave slut", he demanded. Ella dutifully took her master's trousers and underwear off, pulled out his cock and began to suck with a sense of duty greater than most soldiers might feel, giving her master what he thought would probably be, the best blowjob of his life. He felt her wet mouth glide up and down his shaft, and her tongue circling the head in synchrony. It was heavenly for her Master. It was a sensation that he had not felt for a long time. It was such a good blowjob, that he could not hold on much longer, and had to put both his hands on the back of Ella's head, holding her mouth balls deep on his cock while he came down her throat. She tried to pull her head away to breath while she gagged. She had never had a stranger come down her throat before, so she struggled not to swallow the cum that she held in her throat. He looked down at her wild eyes, and then he maliciously said, "Not until you swallow". Realizing again that he was essentially the ruler of her world, and there was no way out of this, she quickly gave in to his demands. "Good. You have learned", he remarked with an expressionless face.

"I know my place Master, it is below you, you don't need to hurt me anymore, I will be a good slut slave for you Master, please don't hurt me!" Ella begged. "Do you really think that I am going to be lenient with my 'slut', or 'submissive'? How little do you think I am Master?", he softly remarked. Ella started trembling in fear as she could see his erection in the distance. Master then continued, "If you try to escape me, I will punish you severely. Do you feel like you've suffered today? Disobey me and you will see what tomorrow brings" He started untying Ella, leading her to believe for a moment that the night was over. He brought her back to her terrifying new reality when he took out a whip and began viciously whipping her back. She screamed out in pain and writhed in pain.

"This is why you are in this situation.", he coldly commented. "You know how I punish my slaves? I make them suffer. I make them cry and I will make you cry. I will punish you for as long as it takes for you to admit to yourself that you are my slave." He brutally brought the whip down on her breasts.

She screeched in pain, and wailed, "I'm a worthless slut!"

"A worthless slut? No, you are a liar, you know very well that I own you." He continued to lash at her back. "And that you are going to be a very valuable slave to me."

"Really? So I am nothing more than your property?" she questioned in tears. "Please stop Master. I will do anything you want, I will do anything you want, I will do anything I can to please you. I want to please you. I CAN please you! Please!"

"Are you a whore?", Master coldly responded. "Are you not happy that you are in my harem? So, what is it that makes you happy? What are you going to do to please me? I can tell you what. You are going to masturbate, right now. You are going to masturbate for me, and I will tell you when you can stop. But you are going to cum. Now stand up", he ordered.

"Thank you Master", she happily responded with a smile. She rubbed her pussy almost forgetting the occasional lashes she received throughout. She became dizzy as she started to lose control of herself and started coming. She cried out as she gushed pussy juice, her squirt almost reaching her master as it arched through the air.

"Very good!" the strange man applauded. "Now, come to me." Ella dropped to her knees and began to crawl on all fours over to where Master was standing. She crawled right up to him and his cock immediately poked out at her. "Feel this slave." He ordered as he stroked himself. He stroked himself while she reached out and began licking the head of his cock. His cries and moans combined into the most ear-piercing sounds as she began to pleasure her new owner. He removed his hand and she stood and began to kiss and suck on his cock. His cock was very thick, and she had trouble getting it all in her mouth. She began to suck on him, and he reached down and began to play with her tits. He moaned as he felt her lips and tongue on his cock, running back and forth between his shaft and his balls. "I'm about to cum!", he told her.

He grabbed her hair and pushed her head down, so that she was literally eating his cock. He came, hard, in her mouth and she was so amazed that she gagged and choked as she began to swallow. The salty taste filled her mouth as she struggled to keep up. He pulled her up to her feet and closer to him, and kissed her passionately as his cock was left covered with his cum. He turned and walked back to his chair. Ella stared at her master in amazement, still not believing what had just happened. She kept her eyes on him as she walked towards the wall.

"There will be no limits on the work you do. You will be my pet, and my slave. You will do whatever I command. You will receive full training as a slave, including anal training. You will obey all orders that I give, and you will please me and satisfy me as I wish."

He then had his way with Ella, several more times. He had to make sure she was really his obedient slut now. He fucked each of her holes. First her pussy, He pounded into it as hard as he could while she moaned and squirmed. He had been surprised by how much she was able to take before he had her in tears. He relentlessly slammed his cock into her until he nearly came again. Then he noticed that it was swollen so he slid his rod from her pussy, and without missing a beat he thrust it into her ass hard. She screamed out with a mix of pain and pleasure as they both came in unison. Master looked down at her and smiled. He was clearly impressed.

The food had just arrived at the table and the ladies hungrily scarfed their food down. Like Ella, Dayna loved playing the submissive role. She had never experienced being the one in charge until recently. She thought of Ella's story and about her experience making someone else submit to her. She tried to decide which of the two made her pussy wetter. Dayna wondered if Ella had any similar experiences.

"Have you ever played the dominant role?", Dayna asked Ella. She shook her head as she imagined what that must be like. Ella had never really considered being the master. Being submissive came so naturally to her and she knew that would probably be out of her comfort zone. Ella was assertive in everyday life, but in bed she was always sweet and obedient.

"Have you?", Ella returned Dayna's question. Dayna blushed a little and nodded her head up and down. Ella tried to picture it but could not conjure up any images in her mind. She glanced at the time on her phone and asked the bartender what time they closed. The bartender informed them that they were closing in about an hour. They went ahead and announced the last call and offered the women another drink. Both shook their heads in refusal and paid their tab, so the bartender left them alone.

"Think you'll be able to drive soon?", Ella asked Dayna. Dayna shrugged looking a little worried. Ella assured her it would be alright. She said they would figure something out if she did not feel good about getting behind the wheel. To pass the time while they waited, Ella suggested Dayna tell the story they had just been talking about. The one about Dayna taking the dominant role. There was just enough time for one more story before the bar closed for the night. Dayna did not feel the alcohol as intensely as before and some of her courage was fleeting. She felt slightly embarrassed about this story but so far Ella had not judged her once, so Dayna decided to tell it anyway. Before beginning the story, Dayna told Ella that it was recent, and she explained that it had happened unexpectedly.

"Get on with the story", Ella said laughing, and knowing this one had to be juicy for Dayna to get so embarrassed suddenly.

"Alright", Dayna replied looking at Ella cautiously.

Dayna Robs the Cradle (MILF)

Dayna entered the principal's office looking clearly frazzled. The school had called and woke her up after she had been working all night. They told her she needed to come to the school but did not say why. She assumed Brady had gotten in trouble. Ever since he turned 8 and started hanging out with different friends he had been getting in tons of trouble. She was at her wits end, and despite many efforts she could not seem to get through to him. He was pulling away from her too. This was heartbreaking because they had always been so close. When all this started, she tried to talk reason into him but after many failed attempts she resorted to punishments, but that did not work either. She saw Brady sitting outside the office looking angry. She walked past him and into Mr. Grayson's office and sat down in the chair across from him. Her stomach sank when she saw the grave look on his face and the thought crossed her mind that Brady might have done it this time. He might be getting expelled.

Mr. Grayson tapped his knuckles lightly against his desk as he spoke, "Ms. Pascal, your son started a fight in the middle of class. Dayna buried her face in her hands and started to plead with Mr. Grayson. She told him getting expelled could really hurt his future and tried to explain that he was a good kid, and that he has just been having a rough time. Mr. Grayson paused to think for a moment. When he spoke again, he told Dayna that he would give Brady one more chance, but only under the condition that Brady join a community outreach program for troubled youth. He explained to Dayna that the program would assign her son a big brother to act as a positive role model. Brady would meet with this big brother and they would do activities together and volunteer in the community. Dayna agreed and even felt that it might benefit her son. She loved the suggestion and made a commitment to take him to the community center and sign Brady up tomorrow when they opened.

After the meeting Dayna walked over and looked at Brady. "Come on", she said to him looking tired and stressed. He got up and followed her to the car without a word. Once in the car, Dayna looked over at her son.

"You've been suspended for two weeks", she told him.

"That's it?" he asked, sounding surprised and a little disappointed. Dayna then began to explain to him that she bartered with the principal to avoid expulsion. She told Brady about the community program and he was immediately infuriated. She firmly told him that he was doing it and that was the end of the discussion. When they got home, Brady went straight to his room and slammed his door. Dayna opened her laptop and began doing research on this program. After seeing what it was about, she felt even more hopeful that maybe it could help her get through to her son. She had tried and every effort only seemed to make him angrier. Dayna enjoyed a long bath, and after setting her alarm, she put herself to bed.

Dayna got up and began making breakfast. She hoped it would improve Brady's mood when she woke him up this morning. She cooked him his favorite, blueberry waffles. She brought a plate to his room. First, she lightly knocked. When she did not get a response, she carefully opened the door. He was laying in such an awkward position that she did not see how it could possibly be comfortable enough to sleep in. She shook his shoulder, and gently called his name till he began to stir. He must have smelled the food because he woke up surprisingly easily. There was usually much more of a fight. When she asked him to get ready, he rolled his eyes but said he would. She felt particularly good because the waffles had paid off. Then she went to her bedroom and began getting herself ready. When she was finished and felt she had achieved the appropriate look for today's tasks, she went to check to see how Brady was getting along. When she knocked on his door, he yelled for her to come in. He was sitting on his bed playing video games as usual. Thankfully, he was dressed and seemed almost ready to go. She told him to come on and he did without a complaint.

They pulled up to the brick building that the brochure for the program had directed her to. She walked in and the waiting room was completely empty. There was a woman behind a window wearing glasses and doing crosswords. Dayna walked up and asked for an application for the program. The woman passed her one through the opening at the bottom of the window and looked back down at her puzzle. Dayna and Brady both took a seat in the waiting room and Dayna began filling out the application, occasionally asking Brady a question that she was unsure how to answer. When she was done, she gave it back to the woman with the crossword, who told her that Dayna would get a call either today or Monday. Dayna nodded and thanked the woman. Then she took Brady back home. As expected, he immediately returned to his video games. Dayna loved that the morning had gone smoothly and without any drama, but she felt very frustrated at Brady's disinterest in hanging out with her. They once had spent time together every day. Now it was hard to get him to say goodnight to her.

Dayna was on the couch catching up on the last few seasons of Game of Thrones when she felt her phone vibrate beneath her. She fumbled for it and managed to hit the answer button just in time. It was someone from the community center who was calling to match Brady with a big brother. The man asked a few questions about the trouble Brady had been having. He asked about the influences in his life and things like his grades and what types of things he enjoyed. After he felt that he knew enough to make a good call, he told Dayna that he had the perfect big brother for Brady. He went on to tell her that he was an eighteen-year-old who enjoyed playing video games and playing drums. Dayna thought learning to play drums would be a great outlet for her son and she committed to buying him a drum set for his upcoming birthday. After hearing Dayna's satisfaction of the match, he asked when was a good time for Jonah to come over and get to know Brady. After the man had called and confirmed that Jonah was available, they had decided on the following day at three in the afternoon.

Dayna went directly to work on getting everything ready for Jonah's first visit to their house. She told Brady, who responded with an expected lack of enthusiasm. She asked her son to clean his room up. He had a bit of an attitude about it, but he said he would. She got started on the rest of the house. She went room by room and made everything spotless. Then Dayna went to the grocery store and grabbed what she needed to make her son's favorite dinner. On her way home she stopped by the local music store. After asking the sales associate a few questions she found a drum set she thought Brady would love. Dayna had not planned to do this, but they offered a fair payment plan, so she put a down payment on the drum set. She returned home exhausted but feeling prepared to make this thing go well. She checked Brady's room and had to give him specific instructions on a few more things he needed to do, but overall, he had everything clean. She went to bed early after a few glasses of wine in front of the television.

The next day she did one more check of the whole house to make sure it was up to her standards, then she began cooking her pizza casserole. It was getting close to three and she had the casserole in the oven baking. Brady miraculously emerged from his room to ask what smelled so good, and she told him she was making pizza casserole for dinner.

"Yum", he said, and for a moment Dayna felt as if she had her son back. She barely heard the knock at the door. She walked to it quickly yelling that she was coming. When she opened the door, Jonah politely held out his hand to her and introduced himself. Dayna shook his hand and welcomed him inside. He was tall and stocky; his brown hair fell in pieces in front of his strikingly green eyes. Brady was right inside, curious to meet the person that the community center had picked to be his role model.

"Hey man, I'm Jonah", he said to Brady who greeted him in return. Jonah asked what video games Brady liked to play and just like that they were off to his room to hang out. Dayna had imagined that her son would be much more reluctant to hang out with Jonah, but he seemed a little excited. When the timer began to beep, Dayna took the casserole out of the oven and sat it on a rack to cool.

She called both boys into the kitchen to eat as she finished putting three healthy-sized portions on three separate plates with a slice of garlic bread. She placed a can of soda beside each plate. They sat down and ate together, which is something her and Brady had not done in a while. Everyone seemed to be enjoying their food. When they finished Jonah thanked Dayna for the delicious meal, and her son surprisingly said thank you as well. Dayna was incredibly happy with how well everything seemed to be going. Before Jonah left, he stopped to speak to Dayna while Brady was in the restroom. He asked if they could set up a time to speak alone about her son. Dayna agreed and gave Jonah her phone number. Brady came out and said bye to Jonah before he left. They scheduled for them to hangout again and play some video games the very next day. After Jonah left, Brady excitedly told his mom all about Jonah. The expression on his face when he told her that Jonah played drums let her know she had made the right call at the music store. She felt like for the first time in a while, she was on the right track with Brady again. Although she had to decide what to do about the one troubling thing she had heard come from her son's room during the visit.

Her and Brady had texted about meeting up and they had decided to meet the following day at a diner to discuss what Jonah is thinking that Brady might need from Dayna. Brady seemed excited about Jonah coming to hang out. Once Jonah arrived, they went straight to Brady's room to play some video games together. Jonah invited Brady to his studio where he practiced playing his drums. Brady asked his mom if she was okay with him coming and she agreed. She was excited that Brady was taking interest in Jonah and not rejecting him just because he was sent by the community center. They had planned to go to the music studio the following week. There were still two weeks left until Brady's birthday, but Dayna went and paid off the drums early and hid them in her walk-in closet, where Brady would not find them. At this point she was sure her son would love the drum set and was overly excited to see his face when she gave it to him.

The time that Jonah and Dayna had scheduled to meet up was only about an hour away. Brady had asked if he could go to a friend's house. She agreed because he had been on the right track since meeting Jonah, but she hoped that allowing him to go did not become a setback. After pondering it, she had decided that not letting him go would be much more likely to cause a setback, so she agreed to let him go. She also thought it might help keep him distracted so she had a chance to meet with Jonah without raising any suspicion. Brady left to go to his friend's house and Dayna got herself ready to meet with Jonah. She arrived at the diner just as Jonah was walking inside. They sat down and both ordered coffee.

Dayna asked Jonah if he was hungry, "My treat", she offered. He agreed after saying that she did not have to. Dayna ordered a breakfast scramble and Jonah got a blueberry waffle. Dayna laughed and told Jonah that was Brady's favorite as well. They talked for a while. Dayna told Jonah about the birthday gift, and Jonah told Dayna that he believes Brady just needs a positive male role model in his life. The diner was noisy as there was a birthday party going on. It had begun to make it difficult for Dayna and Jonah to have a conversation, so Dayna invited Jonah back to the house. When Jonah asked where Brady was, she assured him that he was visiting a friend, so Jonah agreed to go back to the house with Dayna.

On the way back to the house it had begun to rain and then Dayna's car broke down right at the driveway. She began to cuss unsure of what she was going to do to get her car out of the road. Jonah got behind the car and began pushing it into the driveway with seemingly little effort.

She thanked him profusely and he told her it was no big deal. She noticed his clothes were wet from a mixture of rain and his sweat.

"I'm going to need you to take off those sweaty clothes you're wearing. I do not mind drying them off for you. You can use the bathroom". Dayna insisted. He went into the bathroom and began to get undressed. He started with his shoes. Then he took off his wet socks. As he was about to take off his jeans, he noticed her standing by the door, watching him intently. She was now not wearing any clothes from what he could tell, except for a short black robe and the latex thigh-highs which had showed off her very sexy, tattooed legs. He watched her as he removed his jeans, revealing his dark red boxers. He took off his black t-shirt and then turned to find the gaze of a beautiful tyrant. He saw her assessing his body and judging by the way she curled her lip; she was hardly impressed. Her eyes still turned lustful, however.

"Where should I put these clothes, ma'am?", He politely asked.

"Um, you can give those clothes to me, and please do not call me Ma'am, call me Dayna. Ma'am makes me feel old", she said as she gave him an awkward giggle.

He made his way to the couch and watched TV. Dayna made small talk with him every now and then. The storm looked like it was not going away anytime soon. It also made the house look darker than it was. Dayna must have noticed this and decided to switch on the lights and close the curtains. She made her way towards his direction. She placed her knees on the couch and tried to close the curtains behind him. She was right next to him, a small arm length away. He could not help but to stare at her ass.

She may have been very petite, but her ass looked great. His dirty mind wanted to touch it. He wanted to feel what it was like. He may never get another opportunity. What was holding him back was the fear of how she would react to it. She was almost done closing the curtains. It was now or never. He placed his hand on her ass and slowly rubbed both cheeks. She immediately stopped what she was doing and looked at him. Simultaneously, her jaw dropped, and her eyes widened. He rubbed her ass for a good minute. Before she could even ask what he was doing, He told her the worst lie He could think of.

"You had something on your robe, and I was trying to remove it", he said.

"Really?" She asked, looking doubtful.

They both knew it was a lie. Neither of them removed their gaze on each other. He refused to back down an inch from his lie. The silence was brief but felt like a lifetime. Before anyone could speak, the power went off. The storm must have caused a blackout. Without saying a word, she removed herself from the couch and was on her way to her room. She turned and looked at him.

"follow me. I don't want you to sit there in the dark, all alone.", she said. Jonah complied. They entered the master bedroom, with Jonah following her lead. He stood by the door awaiting further instructions. She opened her top drawer by the left counter looking for something. It was her tablet. She turned around and saw me standing awkwardly.

"It's okay Jonah, you can lay on the bed. Get comfortable", she said.

He could not help smiling. For some reason, He thought he must have been forgiven for what he had done earlier. Maybe she saw it as the perverted action of a young boy and decided to dismiss it. He laid on the bed and soon, Dayna followed suit. She slid herself right next to him. She unlocked her tablet and watched a video.

"What are you watching?", he asked her.

"It's a TV show about a young couple who fall in love. Nothing special really", she said.

She slightly turned the tablet to his direction, allowing her to watch with her. It took about 5 minutes for things to get stasis. A good sex scene was being shown. The couple was really going at it. Dayna showed no emotion at all. Jonah, on the other hand, was getting an erection. Without asking, He took his right hand and increased the volume on her tablet. Dayna, holding the tablet, said nothing. He then took his left hand and began massaging his dick underneath his boxers. He was so horny; he did not care that he was doing it in front of a grown woman. She raised her head slightly and saw him massage his dick. She then turned and looked at him. Her brown eyes revealed that she was slightly bothered, but more intrigued. He decided to try a bold move.

"Can you help me?" He whispered.

He removed his five-inch dick from his boxers, took her hand and placed it on his dick. He was hoping that she would do him justice... and she did. She began to massage it. she moved slowly. That was understandable given the fact she was still uncomfortable with what they were doing. But he had a sense that if he played his cards right, he might score a MILF. He placed his hand under her robe and began to massage her right breast. She had small tits. Not like the porn he had seen as he had stroked it many times before. Her nipple was hardening. He kissed her. it did not take long for them to be making out. They did that for about three minutes until he decided to move down her neck.

"Take off your boxers." she instructed. He complied. She rose from the bed and he reached for her skirt, but she stopped him.

"let me do that for you m-m-ma….." he tried. "Master,." she answered for him

She allowed him to pull the robe apart slowly and she revealed a garter belt connected to the thigh highs. She was clean shaven. He turned her around and slapped her ass. She made a soft moan. They then faced each other and shared a deep kiss. Dayna leaned back and opened her toned legs.

"Eat it," she said as if she was asking him to take out the trash for the tenth time. It was music to his ears. He dove in with as much composure as he could muster.
He could not believe he was fucking that dork's mom. He had jokingly threatened the boy with it earlier. Little did he know that Dayna had overheard him say this. She still did not quite trust the older boy completely with her much younger son and had followed them most of the first day. She was not angry at the boy's ego or the cruelty that he had been trying to use on her only son. No, boys will be boys. Dayna saw an opportunity to have her cake and get it eaten out too.
Jonah began to squirm between her thighs which were wrapped around his head like a vice by now. Dayna began

to demand more cock. He jerked his head up gasping for air.

"Fuck me like a big boy." Dayna challenged. He quickly lifted his head and told her to give me a minute and went right back down there. A minute later, He let her have it. He slid in slowly, while looking deep into her eyes, deep into her soul. She was unbelievably tight which surprised him. He would have to pace himself or else he would cum too quick.

"Can you feel it?" Jonah asked. The older woman just looked at him with an arched eyebrow. His motions were slow. He wanted to savor everything.

"Good job." She said, "but I know you can do better than that!" Dayna laughed at the boy. He hastened his thrust. The moans were getting louder. "Faster, Harder!" She screamed.
After five minutes of pounding, the end was near for him. The first round of semen was at the tip of his dick. It was at this moment he realized he did not have a condom.

"Fuck. I am going to cum baby. Where do you want it... AH WHERE DO YOU..."? And he came.
It was all too much. His ejaculation made his legs feel weak and he fell on top of her. she spread her legs as wide as she could. He moaned like a dying animal in the Sahara.

"Wow, whoa", he said.

"I'm glad that you had fun but what about me baby?" she asked.

Dayna had yet to come. She stood up and grabbed him by the hair and forced him onto his knees. She then took his face with her other hand and squished it making the Big Brother's face scrunch up, her nails digging into his face.

She leaned forward and whispered, "Open your mouth, you dirty boy." Jonah complied with gusto. She took a breath in and on the exhale, spat into his mouth. She would be the mentor now.

"Down, now, lay down on the floor. Face up. Now!" Dayna yelled. The boy did as he was told. No matter what. She squatted over his face still on her heels, not yet her with her knees touching the floor and commanded him to feast. The boy did as he was told. Dayna cycled through feeding the boy her ass and her pussy, using his face as a tool for reaching climax. She feared she might have forgotten to let him breath on a few instances and would have to give him mouth to mouth. The boy always came back up gasping for air though. Dayna used him until she had come until she could come no more. Waterfall after gush after squirt drowned the boy but the boy did as he was told. He was hers now.

Dayna gave the boy the key to the back door, telling him that the neighbors watch the front and if they ever saw him, she would punish him but not like this afternoon. The cost for being found out by the neighbors was that he would no longer enjoy the subjugation of "Ms. Slut", as he had taken to calling her. If slave boy were to be seen, she would cut him loose. He could not live with the rejection of his new goddess. They both knew it. As she had commanded, neighbors would never see Jonah again. Nowhere, not even at the grocery store.

He asked if he could fuck her again before he had to leave. "Not yet," she said. "I want to play one more game first. You are going to suck my butt."

The boy stood up and walked over to her as she sat on the couch. "Now that's a good boy", Dayna smiled. He kneeled in front of her, spreading her legs wide and pulling them back. He began licking her and she smacked his cheeks. Jonah did not mind the smacks at all. She grabbed his head and pulled it into her cunt. She moved her pelvis, as she held his head in place, in a motion that rubbed her clit, full labia and finally to rest with his tongue rimming around her asshole before moving again in the opposite direction. She grabbed him by the throat now and forced him on his back again. This time she would use his cock. She had barely begun to grind her wet dripping cunt against him when the boy began to whimper and shudder. She felt as he lost control again. She looked at him and laughed.

"Brief" she said simply. She did not say another word as she moved herself from his cock and onto his face. She didn't get up again until the mess the boy had made was cleaned to her satisfaction.

Ella stared with wide-eyed fascination at Dayna's story. Dayna was still not comfortable driving after she finished telling her story, and the bar was about to close. Ella was happy to offer to let Dayna stay in her hotel room with her for the night. Ella felt she was sober enough to make the drive, especially since it would be a short one, so Dayna could ride with her, and they could come back the next day to pick up Dayna's car so she could get home. Dayna agreed but said she had to text the babysitter first, she still did not trust her son staying home by himself overnight after his shenanigans he pulled whenever he was acting out. She stared down at her phone as she carefully typed out the message informing her sitter that she had gotten too drunk to drive, and that she would be returning in the morning. She had apologized to the sitter and promised her some extra pay for having to stay longer than planned. The sitter texted her back saying that it would not be a problem. As the staff of the bar began to usher the drunks out of the bar, the ladies made their way to Ella's car.

They both got inside, and Ella told Dayna that after hearing her story, she now was interested in trying to be the dominant person, if she ever found the right situation, that is. Dayna looked at Ella and suggested that Ella tell one more story on the ride back to the hotel. They figured it would pass the time better than any radio station could.

"Have you ever been fucked by multiple men at once?", Ella asked Dayna. She shook her head no and told Ella that it had always been a fantasy of hers.

"Well,", Ella began, "your last story was pretty recent, so I think I will tell one of my more recent stories". Dayna nodded her head and adjusted herself in the seat so that she was turned somewhat towards Ella. The two seemed like best friends again at this point. Who knew exchanging sex stories could be such a bonding experience? In a mere twelve hours, it had brought these two ladies closer than they had ever been with anyone else since the time in high school, when they were best friends. In fact, they were probably closer now than they had been then. After a moment of thought, Ella began her story.

Ella Is Outnumbered (Gangbang)

Ella had just started a new job on a design team for a huge real estate developer. She was thrilled to have joined the team. She was nervous about coming in at the end of such a huge project though but from what her manager had said, her team was already ahead of the other design teams in the company. He also informed Ella that the company was offering a genuinely nice paid vacation for the team that won this year's competition. Ella was extremely excited about meeting her team. She understood that she was to be the only female member of this small design team. This made her feel a mixture of both excitement and nervousness. The excitement came from knowing that she could offer the team a more diverse perspective, but she was worried that they might feel superior to her and not accept her perspective. Ella pushed that thought from her mind. She knew she was smart and capable, and surely the other members of her team would be quick to see that, and therefore take her seriously.

Her team consisted of herself and three very accomplished men. Each of them, like her, had graduated from a university with high standards, completed internships at prestigious companies, and has had success in their careers ever since. She walked into the board room overly excited and nervous to meet her team. Ted was the team lead. He had been with the company for the longest out of all the members of her team. In fact, he had completed his internship with them and had been hired right in after his internship. Chang had lots of experience working with various companies in many different countries across the globe. This gave him a uniquely diverse perspective. Lastly there was Blake, who had graduated from an Ivy League College, his resume was fantastic except for a single black Mark that made him somewhat of a liability. Part of this company's culture is to take risks for a chance of big payoffs, they saw value in Blake's experiences that made him unemployable at many companies. Ella was to complete the team. She walked in and shook the hands of each of her new colleagues. She introduced herself and told them what her biggest strengths and weaknesses were. The team mostly seemed to accept her, except Blake who seemed to have some misogynistic tendencies. He was an asshole sometimes and could be hard to work with, but the rest of the team typically had her back when Blake was being disrespectful.

Since Ella had joined the team, they had strengthened and maintained their lead position in winning the paid vacation. She enjoyed working with the team most of the time, and the job paid well. It was demanding though. The men sometimes got a feeling of superiority over her because she was so outnumbered by them, but she was good at standing her ground. This infuriated them sometimes, especially Blake, who would eye her in a way that made her think that he wanted to put her in her place and teach her a lesson. In addition, there were lots of all-nighters, and the lack of sleep sometimes pushed Ella to her limits, but she managed to push through every setback and difficulty and come out on the other side much stronger than she had begun. When the team had received the announcement saying that they had been awarded the vacation, they were not particularly surprised. It was common knowledge that they were leading even before Ella's arrival, and they had only gotten stronger since.

It was their last day of work before their vacation. They had found out last week that they would be taking a trip to a resort in Cozumel that the company had designed the prior year. Ella and her entire team cleared out and cleaned their desks in preparation of their week-long absence. As they left for the day several coworkers extended their congratulations and wished them a fantastic time.

As they were leaving the area of the building where all the design team's offices were, someone yelled, "Bring me back a souvenir". Ella stopped a few times on her way out to say bye to a few friends of hers, including the receptionist who let it slip that she heard they would be staying in the executive suite together. She told Ella that the executive suite was a two thousand square-foot suite with two luxurious bedrooms and a loft featuring three full-sized bathrooms with jetted tubs and enclosed showers. It had a double door entrance and the foyer had Italian marble throughout, and a stunning view. Ella was wowed by Marcy's description of the place she would soon be visiting.

They were going by plane and leaving that same night, so the team met back up at the airport. They received their business-class tickets and were one of the first groups to be called to board the plane. They were seated at the front and as soon as they sat down, the stewardess offered them a pre-flight beverage. Ella noticed Blake eying the stewardess as if she were a meal, and it was obvious that she noticed as well because she avoided making eye contact with Blake for the duration of the flight. All four accepted the offer for beverages and soon the stewardess returned with two red wines, a mimosa, and a beer. They all reclined their seats into a comfortable position as they waited for the pre-flight safety instructions to begin. Soon they were in the air and bound for Mexico.

They landed in Mexico in the early hours of the morning. They all had slight hangovers as they disembarked the plane. A shuttle bus took them and their luggage straight to the hotel where the concierge took their bags and transported them up to their suite. When they entered the suite, they were in awe. Chang looked around the suite in awe with his mouth agape. Ted thanked the design company he worked for as he dove into a king-sized bed with a luscious feather pillow topper. Blake let out a loud whoop to express how pleased he was with their accommodation. Ella walked around the room taking pictures of the beauty and luxury before the guys turned it into a mess. It was not long before the excitement had worn off and they all began to crash. Ella, of course, being the only female, got one of the two private bedrooms. She took the smaller of the two, leaving the larger one for Ted, who was the team leader. Chang called dibs on the upstairs loft and Blake took the pull out which was surprisingly comfortable.

The following day had been planned by their company. They had three excursions to attend and then the remainder of the trip was unscheduled. They set off that morning after breakfast to meet their tour guide at the front of the resort. They first went to the Mayan ruins; they were beautiful, and everyone was in awe of the enormous structures. Next, they got to swim with dolphins in a huge saltwater pool that looked out into the open ocean. Ella loved dolphins so this was an amazing experience for her. She laughed when Blake was too scared of the creatures to even get into the water. The tour guide brought them to a small drive-through restaurant that sold just beans and rice. They did not expect much but they soon discovered that they were the best beans and rice any of them had ever tasted. The last activity that was scheduled was zip-lining. They had a great time, but the mosquitoes were terrible. Everyone in the group was thankful that Ella had the foresight to pack insect repellent to deter them. As per their request, the tour guide dropped them off at a bar just outside the resort. They each had a few drinks before deciding to head back to the resort. On the way back, Ella and Blake got into a heated argument about which way they should go to get back to the resort the fastest.

Ella and Blake tended to bicker quite often. When they were not around, Chang and Ted would joke about the sexual tension between the two. Unknowingly to Ted though, it was him that Ella had an eye for. She had made several attempts to flirt with him which had thus far gone unnoticed. The following day, all four of them began their day with a few mimosas. They walked from bar to bar, occasionally stopping at shops for souvenirs along the way. Once back at the hotel Ella got into the jetted tub to relax with a bottle of wine she had got from a shop while they had been out earlier. Unbeknownst to her, Blake was currently roping the other two men into a scheme he came up with. He figured he would best plant the idea while they were in a drunken stupor, and while Ella was intoxicated as well. Blake had suggested they just ravage Ella the moment she left the bathroom. Chang insisted that they get her approval first because he did not want to risk his job. All three men were very horny, so they agreed to at least try to get her to agree.

When Ella came out of the bathroom in nothing but a robe, she made her way straight to her room. She was surprised to find the rest of her team sitting in her bed waiting for her patiently with a nearly full bottle of tequila and a few souvenir shot glasses sitting between them. They first asked Ella to take a celebratory shot with them. She was already feeling quite buzzed, but she agreed. Ted poured them each a shot and passed them out. Their shot glasses made a pleasant clang as they all came together for a cheer. The shot went down smoothly. Authentic Mexican tequila was far better than the stuff they were accustomed to. Ella was enjoying the conversation they were having about what they wanted to do with the rest of their time here so much that she had forgotten that she was wearing only a towel. Blake was the only one who was brave enough to initiate the conversation that the guys had planned.

"I know something I'd love to do while we're here", Blake said as a naughty grin crossed his face, "Something us guys have decided we'd all like to do". Ella looked at him then at the other two with a quizzical expression.

Blake chimed in again, "We'd like to fuck you, Ella, would you let us fuck you?". Ella was shocked. She paused a moment to process what they were saying.

"You mean all three of you?", she asked, "at once?"

"Yes", Ted chimed in. Her pussy got soaked at the idea, and her face began to become flush. Part of her wanted to say no because she did not want to compromise her work relationships, but she knew she would not be able to do that, she could not resist the temptation. Ted had apparently sensed how nervous their proposal had made her, so he offered her another shot, and she took it gratefully. Out of nowhere Chang began to speak.

"If you don't want to, that's okay", he offered. Ella stopped him by placing her hand on his knee.

"I want to", she whispered breathlessly. She did not know if they heard her clearly, so she slowly nodded her head up and down to let them know that she was a willing participant. She watched as the realization hit all their faces one by one. First Chang looked bewildered. Ted looked excited and ready. Blake looked happy but in a way that made Ella's heart skip a beat.

Ella could not believe she was about to take three cocks in her tight little whore hole in a single fucking. She had dreamed of this day since she had first discovered how much she loved being a slut, while she was in college. Tonight, her filthy dreams get to come true. Her pussy had never been as swollen and dripping with anticipation as it was in this moment. She walked back into the room after going back into the restroom to get herself prepared for what was to come. She showered, and douched her ass, and put her hair into a ponytail. She wondered what plans the men had in store for her. Ella knew Ted had a hard on already. She could clearly see it through his jeans, and she could tell that he was well-endowed. Ella always got lost in his eyes, he was really a handsome man. She clearly recognized the look in Blake's eyes, and it made her shiver. He wanted to fuck Ella up, and he intended to do just that, and she intended to enjoy every bit of it. That lucky bastard Chang would probably cum five times tonight. He had certainly never experienced anything as hot as this. She was gagging at the thought. He certainly seemed happy enough. Her expectations were low as far as he went. She briefly considered the idea that he could surprise her.

Blake started by walking up to her and he glared into her eyes. She squirmed beneath his gaze in anticipation, she started begging him to hurry up and begin. He continued to stand there taking everything in and then a smile crossed his face. He dropped the robe from her shoulders, never breaking eye contact with her. She knew what was going to happen, and she wanted it to. This slut wanted to see her pussy stretched until it could not take any more. Blake pushed her back onto the bed and held her hands above her head, as he signaled for the others to move in. Ted pressed his body against Ella's. He began to kiss her hard, using his tongue to pry open her lips, and forcing it into her mouth as she started kissing him like she was starving for it.

"Fuck!", she thought, "Her nerves were making her tense". She felt so hot. Her nipples were aching. She was dizzy, fumbling with the cuffs Blake had just used to restrain her hands. She pushed her toes hard into the bedpost. Her legs spread wide open with Ted in between them beginning to thrust himself into her pussy.

She could hear metal handcuffs clinking against the top posts of the bed from the force of being fucked. Suddenly, Blake grabbed the back of her head, turning her face towards the side, and rammed his cock into her throat for a moment. Ella wanted to show off a little bit for them tonight, so she began sucking him off with every ounce of effort she had. She was feeling very warm, very wet as Ted buried his rock-hard cock deeper into her. She had always gotten this way around him. In this moment, he was like her sex god and they were his minions. All she ever really wanted was to have him. She groaned in frustration as his hot dick was pulled from her pussy.

"Please...", his lips parted to speak, "I want to hear you scream for me". She begged him not to stop, but he ignored her. Suddenly she was on her stomach with her arms crossed above her, still restrained. Chang was suddenly behind her with his cock out. He pressed his cock against her tight asshole with slowly increasing force until it opened to let him inside. She moaned and pressed back against him. She could hear him panting behind her. Both of her cuffed hands worked hard, massaging the cocks of the other two men who stood on either side of her. Ted shoved his cock into her mouth. She moaned loudly as she noticed the taste of her pussy juices that lingered on his cock. It did not take Chang long to release a gush of cum inside of her ass. The speed at which he was thrusting into her had increased. Both his breathing and his moans had gotten much louder. She heard him grunt and felt his load flow into her as he pressed hard against her. When it was completely done, she felt him relax and heard his breathing start again as he slowly slid his cock from her ass. Then Chang excused himself to the restroom so he could recuperate.

When Ted removed his dick from her mouth, Blake turned Ella's head in the other direction and began fucking Ella's throat again. He pounded his member into her mouth hard enough to make her gag. Meanwhile, Ted pushed his cock back into her still wet pussy. She moaned with her mouth still full of Blake's cock, and she began to squirm against Ted, trying to push him deeper inside of her. She could not believe how good he felt inside of her. She came faster than she knew she could. She felt as if her mind was exploding as Ted continued pushing his cock deeper in her cum-soaked pussy. She could tell Blake was about to come next by the way his boner felt like it was pulsating inside of her mouth. She wondered if he was going to make her taste the cum. She felt Ted's shaft slip out of her suddenly.

"Good girl", Ted cooed as he petted her head, "I want to see you taste Blake's cum". Blake came hard into her mouth, then she looked up at Blake and then at Ted awaiting his praise. She had Blake's cum running down her chin. She wiped her mouth with her arm as Blake undid her cuffs and positioned her in between the two men. In front of her Ted shoved himself back into her pussy, which he seems to have claimed as exclusively his. Blake had begun bucking himself up and down on her already exhausted ass. She screamed out as both cocks filled her holes. This was her first time experiencing real double penetration. It did not disappoint. She immediately felt another orgasm surfacing.

Suddenly, Chang appeared beside her, "show me how much you love my fat cock", he said as he pushed Ella's face down onto his cock. Blake stopped thrusting for a moment, to look at the fully stuffed whore, grinning in admiration of the sight. Ted began ramming himself harder into her and grunting madly. She moaned with orgasmic anticipation, knowing that he was about to fill her with his cum. She felt it gush into her pussy as his body repeatedly slammed into hers. She cried out in gratitude through the throbbing flesh in her mouth. She came again, but this time it gushed from her pussy and soaked the bed beneath her. She fell back onto the bed as they all finished with her and went on to clean themselves up, leaving her panting and whimpering on the bed. All her holes felt stretched to their limit, and she could feel the sticky cum all over her body. She could taste it in her mouth. She lay there panting as sleep overcame her.

Girl Time

Ella whispered the last part of her story so that no one could hear it as they walked across the parking lot and into the lobby of the hotel. The receptionist took Ella's identification and payment momentarily and then returned it with a key card. The receptionist told them where to go and they began walking in the direction as they had been instructed. The hotel was not as bad as Ella had anticipated. It was not what she had grown accustomed to, but it did not give off a trashy vibe, so she was satisfied with it. They came to the door of their room and Ella scanned the key card against the sensor. The light flashed green and they heard the faint click of the door unlocking. They walked inside and looked around taking the place in. Everything looked clean and smelled nice, so Ella plopped on the bed. Dayna plopped down beside Ella who already had the television remote and was putting on a movie. The two friends continued hanging out and chatting with each other, hardly paying attention to the movie.

Ella pulled a bottle of wine and a couple glasses from her bag. She proceeded to pour them each a full glass. They both began sipping the sparkling wine. The bubbles caused Dayna to make a high-pitch noise as she sneezed.

"You're so cute", said Ella, in an offhand manner that makes it sound like it was just an observation.

Ella reached for the remote saying, "After all our exciting conversation, there is no way this movie could possibly hold my attention, so I'm picking something more interesting".

"Oooh, I'm intrigued", laughed Dayna.

Ella hesitated for a moment, gave Dayna a strange look, then took a deep breath. "Okay, then", She presses play on the remote.

They watch for a few minutes. After a while, Dayna felt compelled to mention, "Ella, is this one of those 'so bad it's funny' movies? Because these two chicks can't act for shit."

"It gets better, trust me", Ella stated.

"Okay, because I don't think I'm drunk enough to appreciate it yet", Dayna said laughing.

They kept watching. Then Dayna's eyes got wider and wider as realization dawned. "Ella, this is girl-on-girl porn?"

"Well, it's one of the few things I have yet to cross off my list", said Ella, looking up at the ceiling, "so I guess I have a fixation."

They watched for a little while longer in silence. Dayna became acutely aware of Ella's close proximity, as well as an excited little feeling in her tummy and a disconcerting wet feeling in her panties. She drew her knees together, concerned that the dampness might soak through to her leggings and become a visible wet patch. The silence started to become oppressive — she could even hear Ella breathing beside her — so she spoke up.

"I think I understand. That is one I have yet to mark off my list as well", Dayna said, "But I do have to be home in the morning. I mean I'd love to", Dayna's voice began to trail off as the scene playing out on the television caught her attention. Dayna tore her eyes away from the action on the screen, and briefly glanced at the hand that had started inching up from her knee to her thigh, then she locked eyes with Ella. She found herself unable to look away. Ella is so pretty, and smells so sweet, and she is warm, and she keeps getting closer to me, and I keep getting wetter. Dayna felt herself beginning to lose her resolve.

"I might be able to still make it home early if, if", she stammers as she loses her words, and Ella smiles a victorious smile, and suddenly that hand is alarmingly high on Anna's inner thigh and Dayna's legs are parting almost of their own accord, "Sorry I think watching this is, uh, affecting me", Dayna said.

"Is it having an effect… here?" asked Ella, and her hand was suddenly on that wet place. The place that she had just been worried about Ella noticing the wetness of. She could feel the heat and dampness, and that made her feel encouraged, which turned into desire. She began to lean close to Ella for a kiss. Dayna gasped when Ella's lips pressed lightly against hers, and then her mouth opened to allow Ella's probing tongue inside, exploring the insides of her cheeks. They suddenly fell into a steamy embrace, tasting the sweet wine in each other's mouths. Ella started rubbing Dayna's mound with her whole hand, then graduated to pressing her index finger into the enticing groove she could feel though the leggings Dayna had on.

"Oh fuck", moaned Dayna into Ella's mouth. It was an involuntary exclamation with a couple of meanings. The first meaning being, "this feels so good", and the second, "oh shit, I am about to have sex with my best friend from high school!"

"I have been wanting to do this so bad, all evening" whispered Ella, her soft lips kissing their way around

Dayna's neck and ear as her constantly roaming hand sneaked down under the waistband of Dayna's panties.

Things began escalating more and more quickly. Dayna did not expect to feel Ella's finger go inside her pussy, so she gasped when she felt her soft fingers begin to slip inside her pussy. Dayna felt lightheaded. The look on Ella's face was one of control. Ella slid her fingers out of Dayna and walked across the room. She began digging through her larger suitcase, obviously searching for something. Ella emerged with a small pink backpack.

"I have some toys we can play with", Ella said as she began digging through the bag. She pulled out a strap-on, a leash and collar, a few butt plugs with cute tails attached to them and one that had the word slut on it, a vibrating wand, an odd-looking pink thing, as well as a few paddles and floggers. Dayna's mouth fell open as she looked at all the stuff Ella had brought. Ella insisted that Dayna select the first toy they play with. Ella picked up the odd pink thing, thinking it looked harmless. Ella smiled and asked Dayna to remove her pants. Dayna obediently took her pants off.

"Ready?", Ella asked as Dayna laid back on the bed. Dayna nodded.

Dayna pondered how Ella had suggested they discard their bras earlier in the night, so they could be more comfortable. She now considered, that might have been a clue as to her intentions.

Ella shifted closer, and gently placed the pink thing on Dayna's stiff nipple, then got a leg over so that she was half on top of her friend. She arched her back out as the toy pulled and released her nipple. They kept kissing and Ella started to get a little more passionate, grinding her crotch against Dayna's knee. Dayna's blood was racing, her head swimming, and her pussy creaming itself like crazy. All resistance faded away. Then she grabbed Ella's ass and squeezed it tight as Ella humped her leg. Ella slid the toy down Dayna's body. When she placed it onto her clit Dayna lost all control. Ella giggled as cum began to gush from Dayna's pussy almost instantly.

Dayna's hand slid into the back of Ella's pants, clutching at an exposed ass cheek bared by the skimpy G-string she was wearing underneath. Dayna notices Ella grabbing something from the pile of toys that lay near them on the bed. Dayna felt Ella place something into her hand. Dayna opened her palm and found the butt plug with slut written in red across it.

"I want to eat you," panted Ella, and then Ella slid Dayna's pants over her ankles and positioned herself in between Dayna's legs. Now she was staring down at the top of Ella's head, her bald pussy exposed to Ella's eager gaze, and before she knew it, she had her hand on the back of Ella's head, fingers in her soft hair, as Ella's tongue pressed into her groove. Ella arched her back and got on her knees to elevate her ass into the air and turned in towards Dayna. Dayna took this notion as an invitation and proceeded to wet the butt plug with her spit as Ella continued to eat her pussy. Ella explored deeper, her tongue probing between Dayna's inner lips, then stiffening and jabbing at her entrance, penetrating her and making her shiver. Her nose was pressed against Dayna's little clit, all erect and peeking out from its hood, and she slithered her tongue up to meet it. Dayna tensed, feeling jolts of electricity as Ella's tongue flicked over her bud. Dayna grabbed Ella's ass and slowly pushed the plug into the tight little hole. Dayna flipped Ella onto her back and began to eat Ella's pussy with enthusiasm. Ella loudly moaned in appreciation of the sweet taste. She wrapped her arms around Dayna's neck and her legs around Dayna's head. She wanted it.

"Oh God!" is all Ella could manage before she tensed again, and a wave of pleasure came as Dayna pulled the butt plug from her ass and pushed it back inside. Just as her pleasure was bubbling to the point of orgasm, everything seized suddenly.

"I was so ready to cum!" Ella spits. Dayna smirked playfully.

"And now you're not," she told her, running her fingers through Ella's hair and pinning her eyes with her gaze. "Don't worry, I'm going to fuck you up," Dayna said as she reached down to slip her finger into Ella's pussy. "But I'm not letting you cum without my permission, so be sure to ask". Suddenly Dayna planted her face back into Ella's pussy.

"Oh WOW!" cried Ella. Dayna sucked Ella's clit into her mouth and began to suck, and nibble, and pull. Then Dayna began pounding her fingers inside. An orgasm began to strike her completely unannounced.

"Quickly Ella blurted out, "Dayna can I come?"

"Use your manners", Dayna teases.

"Please?", Ella asked again. Dayna gave her permission to come before beginning to lick it up as Ella began to come. She kept her face pressed between Ella's twitching thighs until it was over, then pulled back and looked up with pussy juice and a grin plastered on her face.

Ella felt her face turning red and she quickly drew her legs up, curling into a ball. Dayna could still see the butt plug sticking out from Ella's ass. "Oh god, oh my god, I can't believe I just did that!" she giggled, hiding her face in her hands.

Dayna got up and hugged her friend, then whispered in her ear. "Do you want to go to bed?"

Ella bit her lip and nodded. "Yeah, I think I'd like to… um… do some other stuff…". Meanwhile, on the television screen, the blonde had tied her 'daughter' face-down on the bed, ball-gagged her and was busy plunging a massive strap-on dildo in and out of her ass.

"So, Ella… do you fancy doing that?" asked Dayna, and they both screamed with laughter.